PIECES OF ME

MISSING PIECES SERIES, BOOK TWO

N.R. WALKER

COPYRIGHT

Cover Art: Covers by Combs
Editor: Boho Edits
Publisher: BlueHeart Press
Pieces of Me © 2020 N.R. Walker
Missing Pieces Series © 2020 N.R. Walker

All Rights Reserved:

No part of this book may be reproduced in any form or by any electronic or mechanical means, including information storage and retrieval systems, without written permission from the author, except for the use of brief quotations in a book review.

This is a work of fiction, and any resemblance to persons, living or dead, or business establishments, events or locales is coincidental. The Licensed Art Material is being used for illustrative purposes only.

Warning

Intended for an 18+ audience only. This book contains material that maybe offensive to some and is intended for a mature, adult audience. It contains graphic language, and adult situations.

Trademarks:

All trademarks are the property of their respective owners.

BLURB

Missing Pieces Series, Book Two

Justin's recovery is slow, but any step forward is a win in Dallas' eyes. Having always been a source of strength for Justin, even before the accident, Dallas is trying to find his feet again as he struggles to get some normalcy back in their lives.

But now, with added financial pressures and Justin's ongoing medical needs, Dallas isn't sure how much longer he can be the strong one.

As missing pieces of Justin's memory return, Justin realises the physical side of their relationship is another piece of the puzzle he desperately wants to put back together. And as he gets to know Dallas all over again, he realises what his mind can't remember, his heart can't forget.

MISSING PIECES SERIES
BOOK TWO

PIECES OF me

MISSING PIECES SERIES
BOOK TWO

PIECES OF me

CHAPTER ONE

JUSTIN

THE MIST WAS thick and heavy, surrounding me and swirling through me, weighing me down. It clung to my bones and made it hard to move. Heavy and tiring, and impossible to see through. If I could just see past it, through it, if it would just clear a little, I'd be able to see . . . All the answers were in there, the life I'd had, everything I'd known, was shrouded in mist . . .

Until the wings came into view. Like they had before in every other dream. Hard to recognise at first, so much was missing. But they shone a little brighter now, the mist swirled and danced around the wings, and I tried to get to them faster. I needed to be closer, and the mist began to clear. I reached out and touched the wings. I'd never been able to touch the wings before . . . This was new, and I was closer than I'd ever been.

Then the mist was gone.

The wings were soft under my palm. A heartbeat boomed under my touch, scaring me. Calling me home.

I startled awake with a name echoing through my head.

Dallas.

And for a brief moment, I could feel his warmth, his strength. I could smell his scent, taste his kiss . . .

Then it was gone.

I closed my eyes, trying to grasp what was left of that dream, trying to recall every detail, but I couldn't. The dream I'd had many times had changed now I knew what the wings were. What they meant, and why they felt like home. When I had no idea what home even was, those wings resonated in my heart.

I understood now why that stranger who sat by my bed in the hospital, who never left, felt so familiar. I didn't know him, I'd never seen him before, but for some reason I trusted him. When he'd held my hand in hospital, it felt . . . right. It felt new, but somehow familiar.

And now I knew why.

Sure, I'd seen the photos of us together, and I'd read the text messages, but they never sparked any feeling apart from sadness, because I couldn't remember, and I longed for what the two guys in the photo had. I had no emotional connection to those pictures. I didn't recognise him in those photographs, and I didn't recognise who I was in them either.

But somewhere in my brain, in the mist and blank confusion, was a pair of wings—a memory—that had been trying to tell me since the accident that the man by my bedside was my home.

I'd had snippets of memories, of things I knew, but this one was a big one. This one had feelings behind it. Safety, comfort, strength.

Like he'd said, if that was the only thing I ever remembered, he'd be happy with that. And I kind of agreed with him. I mean, I wanted all my memories back, but that one was a real good place to start.

I pressed the incline button on the couch and sat up, giving myself a few seconds to adjust. I hated how my body and my mind were no longer in sync. How it took a few seconds for things to register, like there was a two-second telecast delay. And the worst part was that I knew I was talking slow. I could hear it, but I just could not kick my brain into second gear. Everything I did was slow. How I thought, how I spoke, how I moved.

It was just how I was now.

I hated it, but there was nothing I could do about it. Sure, it was frustrating, but I just didn't have the energy or the brainpower to be angry about it. There were a lot of things my mind wouldn't let me do. A lot of things I knew I should care about or ask about, but I just . . . couldn't. I didn't have the capacity for it.

I could remember what it was like to be thinking about twenty different things at once, to worry about things like work and money, but now my mind had none of that noise.

There was only mist, and haze, and a whole lotta blank.

At least my bladder still had a direct line to my brain. With a sigh, I sat forward on the couch and got myself onto my scooter. I used the bathroom, then sat in front of the jigsaw puzzle for a bit. I got some more of it done, which felt good. It was slow-going like everything else, but it felt good to accomplish something. Progress was progress, one piece at a time.

Dallas came up for lunch and he was all smiles when he saw me at the table. "Hey, you."

My belly did a little somersault, and the pleasantness was a nice change from the confusion that I'd been shrouded in. "Hey."

He came over and put his hand on my shoulder. It was

warm and there was a gentle strength in his touch. "Getting more done, I see. It's looking really good."

I didn't know why his approval meant a lot to me. I smiled up at him. "Thanks."

"I'm gonna make myself a toasted sandwich. Want one?"

Food. Did I want to eat? I thought about my stomach and if it was hungry, but I couldn't really tell. If Dallas was eating, then I probably should too. "Sure."

He set about getting the toaster thing out, then bread and other stuff from the fridge. I left the table and scooted over to the kitchen, and remembering where the plates were, I put two plates on the counter.

Dallas grinned at me. And instead of making a fuss about me doing stuff, he talked about the bikes they were working on: one was a simple service, one needed a new brake line, and another was having the forks replaced because the guy had stacked it hard in the national park up north. "Sorry if the noise down there is disturbing you," he said. "Did it wake you up?"

I had to think . . . "Nope. Didn't hear anything." Had I heard anything? I knew how loud mechanic shops could get with motors kicking over every so often, things banging and clanging . . . How could I not hear that? I was right above it . . . "Haven't heard anything."

"Well, good," Dallas said. "I wondered if we were disturbing you."

I put two bottles of water on the counter, trying not to think too much about me not hearing loud noises outside. "It's weird," I said. "My head is blank most of the time. Like really misty and empty, but it's full. There's no more room. I can't think about stuff because all the space is taken up by mist. That probably doesn't make sense, sorry."

"It makes perfect sense," he said, that kind smile everpresent. "It's probably a good thing you can't hear it. Especially Sparra's singing."

I smiled at that and Dallas slid the toasted sandwiches onto the plates, then took them to the table, careful of the jigsaw puzzle. "Let's see who gets the next piece."

I carried the waters from the counter as I scooted over and Dallas sat next to me and slid a plate in front of me. "Careful, these'll be a bit hot. Might want to leave it for a bit."

"'Kay." I picked up a puzzle piece and slotted it into place.

Dallas gasped. "You cheated!"

I laughed. "Did not." I had all the same colours put together. "I've just been looking at it longer."

He grumbled and picked up a piece but couldn't get it to fit. "Oh, this is bullshit," he said with a chuckle.

I sorted through the pieces near me and gave it to him. "Try that."

It slotted straight in and I laughed. "Okay, you win," he said, giving me a full grin. "So I was thinking about this date tonight."

Date . . . oh yeah. "Our second first date."

"Yep. I was thinking we could order some Chinese food for dinner and start watching *Game of Thrones*, make some popcorn, and maybe if I'm real lucky, we could hold hands."

I was smiling at him, that giddy feeling was back. "Hold hands, huh?"

He chewed on his bottom lip, looking all kinds of cute and happy. "How does that sound?"

"Good." I know he said a few things—Chinese food and TV—but one stuck out more than the others. "I like holding hands."

He laughed and picked up his sandwich, then nodded toward mine. "These are fine to eat now."

"Okay." I took a bite, and it was good. I liked mustard and it was helpful that I didn't have to tell him what I liked, because if I tried to think too hard about what food I liked and didn't like, I couldn't name them. Everything was harder when I was tired, and I was tired all the damn time.

I wanted to try harder, though. I wanted to be better. I just needed to try and wade through the mist and make sense of what lay beneath it.

"Oh, and I called the hospital," Dallas said between bites. "Eight o'clock tomorrow you can get your cast off. Arranged it so it's before your appointment to see your PT doctor and Doctor Chang."

Ugh, more appointments, but at least I was finally getting rid of the cast. "Thank you. I can't wait to have it off." I looked down at my arm. "I want my body back. I hate not being able to . . ." What was the word? I couldn't quite find it. ". . . move and stuff."

"Tomorrow you'll be new and shiny." Dallas' smile became a frown. "Though tomorrow's gonna be a pretty full-on day. Lots of appointments and walking about. Will you be okay with that?"

Probably not, but if Dallas was with me . . . "You'll be there, right?"

"Of course." He stood up and rubbed my shoulder before taking his plate to the sink. "I wouldn't be anywhere else."

He sat back down at the table but looked through the puzzle pieces while I ate my sandwich. Everything I did was so damn slow. And it never fazed him one bit. He never made an issue that I took so long to eat or talk. He was just so great about everything.

"A-ha!" he said, slotting a piece into place. "I got one."

I smiled as I chewed, and without really meaning to or without thinking about it, at least, I reached for his hand. I just wanted to hold it, apparently. And he laced our fingers with a grin and proceeded to look for another puzzle piece.

He stayed for a bit longer, and I really loved having him here. His warmth and his scent and his hand in mine, it settled something in me. The confusion in my head was calmer when Dallas was there, and I knew he'd look after me and he'd make sure everything was okay. I knew he couldn't stay with me all day, but it was good to see him, to be with him.

"Well, I better get back downstairs. I told the boys I'll be out all day tomorrow," he said. "So I better get as much done today as I can." He leaned down and kissed the top of my head and headed toward the door.

"Dallas?" I called out. Damn my stupid brain . . . In the three seconds it took for me to stop him, he was almost gone.

He turned. "Yeah?"

I pushed my scooter out from the table and stood up. "Can I . . . ugh, can I have a hug?"

He crossed the floor in a few long strides and collected me in a crushing hug that was everything I needed. God, it felt so good. He was a good six inches taller than me and much stronger, so he could just wrap me up and, my God, he just made everything so much better. It was like he transferred some of his strength to me, which was ridiculous, but I felt stronger after he hugged me. Some of his calmness settled over me.

That shit was like a drug.

I breathed him in and would have stayed right there forever if he didn't pull back. There was concern in his eyes. "You okay?"

I nodded, smiling now. "You give the best hugs."

He chuckled. "You can have one any time."

"Good."

He was warmth and strength, and I fit against him just right. His hands were big, his skin rough and calloused and divine. When he cradled my face, I couldn't help but lean into his touch.

He studied my eyes for a long moment before he pressed his lips to mine. Just quick, but soft and warm, and his beard tickled my chin. "I better go back downstairs," he said quietly. "Call me or text me if you need me, okay?"

"'Kay."

I took my plate to the sink and washed up the few things we'd used. It wasn't much, but I wanted to help as much as I was able, and it probably wasn't the best job. Washing up with one hand, and my left hand at that, wasn't easy. But I got it done and felt better for it.

Then I parked my arse back on the couch and picked up my journal. Writing with a full-arm cast was bad enough, and even I could tell my writing was bad, but I managed to write down what I remembered about the wing dream and about Dallas' tattoos. I wrote down that I knew about the fridge and the radio downstairs, and I wrote down that I'd had another nightmare.

But then I also made a list, trying to write it as neat as possible, of the things I wanted to remember to talk about. Things I knew I should talk about but didn't really have the capacity to. I figured if I made a list, then when I was actually able to, I could ask. I wanted to be better for Dallas, and for me too. But I wanted to get better—I wanted to have the life the old me had in those photographs with him. I wanted that. And that meant I needed to think harder, to try harder to get my life back.

But the whole time my mind just kept going back to Dallas.

And in an attempt to find some answers, or maybe in hope that I'd see something that would open the locked vault of my memories, I got myself back onto my scooter and went to the end of the hall.

Dallas' bedroom.

CHAPTER TWO

DALLAS

ACCOUNT OVERDUE.

Past due.

Insufficient funds.

I sighed and stared at my laptop screen. Between the guilt and shame was an overwhelming sense of drowning. Even when I'd first started my business, I'd never had money worries. Not like this. Now bills were coming in that I couldn't pay, and orders weren't delivered because I couldn't pay upfront, so I was swapping money between accounts, playing cat and mouse with debtors and creditors just trying to keep my head above water.

I typed out another quick email asking my case manager to please chase up the workers' compensation and insurance claims. It had only been a few weeks since we'd filed the paperwork, but our workload had lessened to almost half, yet the bills had never stopped coming.

I'd never kept anything from Justin before, but he couldn't know about this. It would only add to his stress and be detrimental to his recovery.

I closed my laptop and sighed. I'd promised Juss some

Chinese food for dinner, so I added that to my growing credit card debt and shut my office door.

After Davo and Sparra had gone, I locked the workshop up, padlocked the front gate, and carried the Chinese takeout up the stairs. Despite the worry about money, I was excited for tonight. A night on the couch in front of the TV probably sounded lame to anyone else, but it sounded kinda perfect to me.

All the little things I once took for granted were now like pockets of gold. Watching TV, curling up on the couch, holding hands . . .

I would never take them for granted again.

It had very nearly all been taken away from me, and now I knew its true value, I'd never discount anything ever again.

The loungeroom was empty, so I put the Chinese food on the kitchen counter and saw the bathroom door was open. "I ordered dinner early," I said. "So I didn't have to leave again."

No reply.

I walked to the bathroom and peeked inside, half expecting him to be at the basin or peeing or something.

He wasn't.

Trying not to panic, I turned to his bedroom. Maybe he'd gone for a proper lie-down, but his bed was empty.

I called out louder this time. "Juss?"

It was then I noticed the door to my room was ajar. *What the hell?*

I peered in, almost afraid of what I might find, my heart in my throat. But there he was, asleep on my bed.

Oh, Jussy.

My heart was doing all kinds of crazy things, trying to calm down after almost having a panic attack but filling with love and sadness. Why my bed? Had he needed to be close to me?

I quietly sat beside him and put my hand on his arm. "Hey, Juss."

He stirred awake, drowsy and confused at first, until he noticed me. "Oh, hey."

"You okay?"

"Yeah, why?" He sat up and looked around. It clearly took him a few long seconds to remember. "Oh."

"Were you looking for me?"

"No, I . . ." He shook his head. "I didn't mean to fall asleep. I want to be better. For you. And I thought maybe if I saw your things, I might remember . . . But I was tired."

I slid my hand up his arm. "You want to be better, for me?" I shook my head. "Juss, you don't have to do anything for me."

"I want to." He squeezed his eyes closed and scrubbed his hand over his face. "I want to be better."

"It'll take time," I whispered, taking his hand. "And baby, we've got time."

"Do we?"

I nodded. "All the time in the world."

He sighed and looked around the room. "This isn't your room, is it?"

"Sure it is."

"I mean, you said it was your room, and you said I needed a private room."

He was frowning, so I clarified, "I didn't want you to feel pressured, that's all. Bringing you home to share a bed with a man you didn't know kinda felt wrong to me."

He looked at me then, smiled, and shook his head. "There's no bed in here."

"There's this," I said, patting the thin mattress we were sitting on.

"It's a sofa bed, not a real bed."

"You slept on it okay."

"It smells like you."

I smiled at that, and he threaded our fingers. "You can take naps in here whenever you like."

"It's a small room," he said, looking at the desk, the old printer, and the very lack of anything else. There was no room for anything else. I had to step over the sofa bed to get to the desk. "It's not a bedroom."

He didn't say anything about the small pile of clothes folded on the desk that I was using as a dresser, or my joggers under the desk. "It does me just fine."

"Does it make you sad?" he asked. "To sleep in here?"

Jesus. I wasn't prepared for this conversation. I lifted his hand to my lips and kissed his knuckles. "No, Juss. I'm glad to have you home. That's enough for me."

He was quiet for a minute, and I let him get his thoughts in order. "What time is it?"

"Almost six. I had some Chinese food delivered already. You hungry?"

"Uh, sure." Then he smiled. "It's our date night."

I chuckled. "It is. Here, let me help you up." I stood and held out my hand. "Where's your scooter?"

He took my hand and put his feet on the floor and slowly stood up. "I left it in the hall. There wasn't enough room in here."

I hadn't even noticed it; I'd been in such a panic to find him. But he took a few steps on his own, with me holding onto him, and he walked to the door. I was grinning at his progress, at his determination. "How does that feel?"

"Okay. Weird. Sore. But good." He held onto the doorframe. "Feels good to be up."

"Well, just don't overdo it," I said, grabbing his scooter. "Or you'll end up back at square one."

He sat on his scooter and sighed. "I shoulda stayed upright. I need to pee. Now I gotta get up again."

I chuckled. "Well, I'll leave you to do that and go sort dinner out."

By the time he came out, I had dinner on the table, careful of the jigsaw puzzle, of course, with two cans of lemon soda and two empty wine glasses. I also had the lights down low and two candles lit on the table.

He stopped and stared; a slow smile tugged at his lips. "What's this?"

"A date," I replied. I felt a bit foolish, actually, but I wanted to do something special. And corny, because Justin had always liked corny. No, we weren't fancy, and no, our wine glasses weren't expensive crystal, and the candles were just the old ones I had in case of a blackout. But all Justin had ever wanted was a guy who made him feel special, and given the circumstances, this was as special and as corny as I could do. "Our second first date. This isn't too corny, is it?"

He grinned as he scooted over to the table. "This is great." Then he laughed. "I can't believe you did this."

I poured the drink into his wine glass. Alcohol was out of the question, given his brain injury, so a non-caffeinated soft drink it was. "For you, sir," I said, taking my seat.

He was still grinning as he sipped it. "Did you do this before?" he asked. "I mean, did you do this for me before?"

"Candle lit dinners? No, actually, I didn't. This is a brand-new memory for you. A first." We'd had nice dinners at home before, plenty of times, but I'd never lit candles and used wine glasses with Chinese food before. "I should have, though. I should have done it all the time, and now I can't think of one single reason why I didn't."

Justin's smile became something else. Happier, a little shy, and somehow just for me.

It set the butterflies in my stomach to full flight. I wiped my hands on my thighs and let out a laugh.

"What?" he asked, a faint blush on his cheeks.

"Just you." I shrugged. It was scary how it had almost been taken away from me and I never wanted to ever take it for granted again. But I didn't want to dampen our date night with constant reminders of his accident. "You're just really cute, and I like seeing you happy."

He laughed it off with a roll of his eyes, embarrassed. So I eased up on the compliments and dished out the food instead. I'd ordered his favourites, but nothing too spicy, and there would be enough leftovers for tomorrow.

"I didn't mean to fall asleep in your bed," he said on his way to taking a sip of his drink.

"Oh, that's okay. Don't think anything of it." The truth was, it was kinda nice that he was thinking about me and trying to make sense of our relationship when I wasn't there. He was trying to fill in so many blanks. "Is there anything you wanted to know about me?"

"Well, yeah," he said. "Everything. I don't know anything about you. Not really. I know you're nice. And kind. And I know I trust you, and I like you," he said, then cleared his throat. He made a face and his blush deepened. "Like, I *like* you. You give the best hugs that heal something in me, so I'm guessing my heart knows the real you, so I should probably get my head caught up."

I stared at him, almost not believing what he was saying. It made me so ridiculously happy that I wanted to pick him up and twirl him around like some stupid romance movie.

Instead, I gave his hand a squeeze before I shoved food into my mouth so I didn't grin like a crazy man.

He wanted to know everything, and considering this was his first date with me, I started at the beginning. "I was born in Singleton, went to school there. Got a mechanical apprenticeship when I was seventeen; couldn't get out of school fast enough. Moved to Newcastle when I was nineteen and finished my apprenticeship at Yamaha."

He made a face as he chewed and swallowed his mouthful. "Yamaha . . . shame."

I laughed at that. "Sorry it wasn't with KTM."

He smirked. "I knew you couldn't have been *that* perfect."

I chuckled at this side of him. This was the old Justin. The Justin who joked and took the piss out of me every chance he got. "I have two older brothers, Dean and Mark; they both live in Singleton still. I don't talk to them too often. My mum died when I was eight and my dad remarried when I was thirteen. No one really liked the fact I was into guys, and no one really cared too much when I left town."

He put his fork down. "Oh, Dallas, I'm sorry."

"Don't be. It's what made me who I am today. I decided the best revenge was success, and I own my own business, I own this place. It's not the Taj Mahal, but it's mine. It's more than what they have."

He reached over and took my hand, and frowned. "My mother doesn't like me either."

I squeezed his fingers. "I know, baby. But you've got Becca and the girls, and you've got me. And I've got Davo and Sparra. They're like my brothers. We get to make our own family and I'll take that any day over a shitty biological one."

He nodded. "Did we . . . was that something we had in common?"

"Yeah. One of a lot of things, but it's something we both understood."

"What else?"

"What it was like to be a gay mechanic," I said. "It's not an industry that is all too tolerant of that kind of stuff. And other gay guys, in clubs and stuff, never really stuck around. Guess they didn't like oil-stained hands or something."

"Do your customers know about us?" he asked. "I mean, did they know we were . . . ?"

"Our regulars know. If it bothered them, they'd have gone somewhere else, I guess. But just the typical customer, nope. None of their business, really."

His smile was kinda sad, and he was staring at our joined hands on the table. "You know, I like a mechanic's hands. Your hands. The grease and . . . it gets into the nails and the skin." He turned our hands over and looked at my nails. "They're not pretty. They're banged up and rough, but these hands work, and they fix things, and that's pretty great."

I stared at him in the flicker of candlelight and my heart fell a little more in love.

"You're looking at me like that again," he said. He took his hand back and picked up his fork—I kind of forgot he only had one hand to use—and he ate some more food.

"Like what?"

"Like you know me . . . like you like me." He made a face and stabbed a piece of plum chicken with his fork.

"Does that make you uncomfortable? I'm sorry. I don't mean to. I just . . . can't help it sometimes."

He smiled around his mouthful of food. "No, I don't

mind." He met my gaze. "It's better than the sadness. I didn't like that much."

"Sadness?"

"Yeah, at the hospital. You used to look sad when I didn't know who you were."

"I never was much good at hiding the way I feel."

He ate some more. "Did I like that? That you couldn't hide the way you feel? Pretty sure that I'd have liked that."

I chuckled. "Yeah, you liked that. Even if we had a fight, you'd tell me afterward that you'd prefer to know and not have the mind games."

"Did we fight often?" he asked with a frown.

"Not really. Usually it was over stupid stuff, like dishes or laundry or not replacing the empty toilet paper roll. Stuff that really doesn't matter at the end of the day. We never had any major disagreements."

He surprised me by laughing. "Toilet paper?"

I chuckled, considering he almost died and we wasted precious moments arguing over fucking toilet paper. "Crazy, huh?"

He smiled as he ate. "Tell me more about you."

"Like what?"

"I don't know. I can't really think of questions. What would people on a first date ask?"

I took a long sip of my drink. "Well, let me see . . . My favourite colour is blue. Favourite food is a big dirty burger from the takeaway shop down the road. Never was a big drinker, but if the boys were having a night, I'd probably have a Jack and Coke. I like watching the footy; I'm a Bulldog supporter as you know."

He groaned. "So bad."

I laughed. "I like the Sydney Swans in AFL, the Newcastle Jets in soccer."

"Those are okay. I can deal with those. But the Bulldogs . . ."

I rolled my eyes and smiled as I ate some Singapore beef. "And when the Bulldogs played the Knights, we'd have a bet. It was usually just like washing up for a week or a foot massage, something like that."

He grinned. "So, how many times did you lose that bet?"

I pouted. "Shut up."

He laughed at that. "See? I can lose five years and I still know the Knights beat the Dogs."

I pushed my plate away. "We won a few."

He gave me a happy smile, then nodded to my meal. "Do I like that?"

"Try it."

He pierced a piece and hummed as he ate it. "I like that. I've never had that before, have I?"

"Yep, you have."

He frowned. "I don't remember it. It's weird that I've done things, eaten things, lived a whole life that I can't remember."

"It must be very weird," I replied. "And I can't pretend to understand what it's like for you. But I'll help you, and if you have any questions or want to know anything, I won't ever lie to you."

He met my eyes and smiled. "Thanks. It can't be easy for you either."

"I dunno," I replied, giving him a nudge. "I get to do it all again with you. I get a second chance to make everything better."

He seemed to think about that for a long moment. "What would you do different?"

"Well, I certainly won't be arguing about toilet paper, I

can assure you."

He smiled. "Glad to hear that."

"I won't sweat the small stuff. I'll appreciate the little things and I'll never take a single day for granted."

He studied me. "The accident scared you," he said. It wasn't a question.

"Terrified me." I tried to smile. "Terrified me."

"It musta sucked. Sorry."

"Not as much as it sucked for you," I said, getting to my feet. I rubbed his shoulder, then began to clear away the table. "Want to go get comfy on the couch? This'll just take a second."

"Sure." He scooted a plate to the counter. "Um, I know you said something about watching a TV show . . ."

"Yeah, but we don't have to."

"I just can't concentrate too much, sorry."

"That's okay. You can choose what we watch. I don't mind at all."

By the time I finished cleaning up, Juss was on the couch flipping through the sports channels so I blew the candles on the table out and joined him and Squish on the couch. Again, I sat close but not too close and within a few moments, he'd wiggled over. He had always been like a koala, clinging and touching, and I certainly didn't mind one bit.

We watched a replay of last season's football grand final but it wasn't even into the second half when his head was on my shoulder and his blinks were getting longer and longer. "Wanna go to bed, baby?" I asked.

"Tired," he said. "Always tired. Wish I wasn't."

"You need to sleep," I said gently. "Your brain is recovering."

He was quiet for a bit. "You call me baby. Or Jussy."

"I do, sorry. It's a habit."

"What'd I call you?"

Such an innocent question, but damn, it hurt my heart a little. "You'd call me Dall. Short for Dallas. Or babe. Not in front of the boys at work; just when it was us."

He hummed sleepily. "Like that."

Me too, baby. Me too. And maybe one day we'll get back to that.

I got him up to use the bathroom and I got him his meds and he was almost asleep when I helped him into bed. He mumbled something that I couldn't understand, and with a deep breath, he was out like a light.

I leaned down and kissed his head, right next to the scar above his ear. "I love you, Jussy," I whispered, knowing he was asleep. I wanted him to know, even on a subconscious level, that he was loved.

Squish quickly joined him, like he always did, curling up at his side and purring loudly, and I left him in charge. I got everything tidied up and went to my room, smiling at the rumpled blankets where Justin had slept. I inhaled the faint scent of him as I settled into sleep. I'd barely dozed off when Justin's voice woke me.

"Dallas?"

I shot up, wondering what was wrong. I got to his room, and he was sitting up in his bed. "Can't sleep," he mumbled, then pulled the covers back in invitation.

I didn't need to be told twice. I slid in between the sheets, and before my head was on the pillow, he was snuggled into my side. I rolled and pulled him against me, his head against my chest, and he mumbled again, but this time I heard him just fine.

"Don't leave me."

CHAPTER THREE

I WOKE up with Justin plastered to me. He was snuggled right in, his heavy cast across my belly, his thigh across mine. Once upon a time it might have been annoying, waking up with a heat-seeking koala wrapped around me, but now I relished it.

My body liked it too.

Needing to pee didn't help, but having him so close after so long . . . my body *definitely* liked it.

He was sound asleep, and I figured it would be best if he didn't wake up with my persistent dick staring right at him. I'd crawled into his bed wearing only my boxers, so there wasn't much hope of hiding it.

I gently lifted his leg off mine. It was his injured leg so I had to be careful, and when I slipped out from under his arm, he stirred but never woke. Once out of bed, I took a second to watch him sleep.

Fucking hell, he was gorgeous.

His injuries reminded me that he was vulnerable, but by God, he was resilient and strong too. And sexy as hell.

My dick agreed, which reminded me to leave before he

saw me. I used the bathroom and I tried to think of every-thing we had to do this morning, listing his appointments in my head, but my problem wasn't going away on its own.

Shower first it is, then.

Jerking off hadn't been something I'd done much of since Justin's accident. I'd either been too tired, too distracted, or too heartsore. But now that he was home and sleeping in the same bed seemed to be something that might happen often, I figured I should probably get used to it.

It didn't take much . . . the hot water, a soap-slicked hand, and memories of Justin and me and the countless nights of frenzied fucking or gentle lovemaking, of being buried inside him, making him come just from having my cock inside him. God, how he loved that . . .

It didn't take much at all.

I finished my shower, feeling a little lightheaded and much looser. I dressed and went to the kitchen and put the kettle on. I was making some toast when Justin came out on his scooter. He looked still half-asleep.

"Morning," I said brightly.

He grumbled and I handed him his coffee. He never was much of a morning person, and seeing this familiar side of him made me smile. "You always so chipper in the morning?"

"Yep. And you're always cranky. Actually, never thought I'd miss seeing you scowl at me first thing in the morning until you did it just now. I've missed it." It was a sure sign he was improving.

He grumbled something else as he sipped his decaf coffee.

I had to bite the inside of my cheek so I didn't grin. "Cast comes off today. That's gotta be a good thing, right?"

He didn't grumble, so that was a yes.

He became a little more human with every sip of coffee and each passing moment. He ate some toast, and by the time he was showered and dressed, he was his usual smiley self. I raced his scooter and his papers down first, then helped Justin down the stairs, and he laughed as I helped him into the ute.

And he was still smiling as we arrived at the hospital, though I was fairly sure he wouldn't be smiling by the time we left. It was going to be a long, gruelling day for him.

He stopped at the entrance of the hospital, looking up from his scooter to the sign above the door. "Not too keen to come back here," he said.

"Me either," I admitted. "I must have walked through these doors a hundred times in the last month."

"Just promise me one thing," he said very seriously.

"Anything."

"We won't have lunch here. No more hospital food, ever. I don't care if they're giving it away."

I laughed. "Promise."

We made our way to the plaster clinic and went through all the paperwork, and thankfully we didn't have to wait too long. Justin was adamant that I was going with him, so I sat and watched as they cut his cast off. His arm was paler than the rest of him and thinner than his left arm. He had final X-rays done, and he had to wear one of those collar-cuff things, which just kind of kept his hand tucked up to his chest. The bone from his shoulder to his elbow still needed to sit right for another week or so, but at least the collar-cuff wasn't heavy and cumbersome like the full arm cast.

"How does it feel?" I asked as the nurse fitted his hand into the cuff thing.

He smiled at me. "Much better. Can't wait to have a

shower and scrub it." He ran his fingers along his forearm. "Why isn't it itchy now? So not fair."

"No doubt the doc will have a whole lot of exercise and physio for it too," I said.

He grimaced. "More homework."

"Well, at least they let you leave. You could still be doing all this from your hospital bed."

"Yeah, no thank you," he said. "I'm done with hospitals forever."

"You *are* done," the doc said, giving him a big smile. "Well, you're done here." She gave him a few tips and pointers about his arm, but I didn't think he was listening. His mind was already out the door.

His physical therapy appointment was with a new out-patient doctor. Doctor Michaels seemed nice enough, though he gave me a questioning look, obviously wondering where I fit into Justin's care. But as soon as Justin trans-ferred himself from his scooter to his seat, he reached over and took my hand. "This is Dallas," Justin said to him. "He'll be sitting in with me." I grinned at Justin—that was a pretty ballsy move for him—and he squeezed my hand in response.

The doc just smiled. "Okay then, let's get started."

The appointment itself was more of an introductory thing. Sure, he had Justin's file and could read all about his injuries, but he was more interested in observing and listen-ing. He had Justin show him his range of motion in his leg, and now that his arm was out of his cast, he showed him what strengthening exercises he could do. Justin's daily routine was mostly all from a sitting or lying perspective because dizziness was a factor with brain injuries, and fatigue, of course.

By the time we were done, Justin's blinks were getting a

little longer. It might not have been too noticeable, but I saw it; he'd had enough. And, of course, we had to wait for Doctor Chang—she was busy with patients on the ward. When she came into the waiting room to call us, she took one look at us with Justin's head on my shoulder while he rested his eyes, and she grinned.

"My two favourite customers," she said quietly.

Justin sat up, blearily trying to get his bearings. "Oh, hey."

"You up for this appointment?" she asked him.

"If it means I don't have to come back," he replied. A guy in the waiting room laughed and Doctor Chang rolled her eyes.

"Come on through."

"It's been a busy morning," I said once we were in her office. "First appointment was to get the cast off his arm. Then we met the new physical therapist, so we had to show him where we're at. And now we're here."

She gave me a nod, then turned her attention to Justin. "How're you feeling, Justin?"

"Yeah, I'm good. Just tired 's all."

"Is it good to be home?"

"Yeah," he answered. "I remembered a few things."

"Excellent," she said with a smile. "And you brought your journal?"

"Oh yeah," he said. He looked at the papers I was holding for him. "Babe, the journal . . ."

Babe.

He called me babe.

"You can talk about what I wrote," Juss said. "In front of Dallas, I mean. I don't mind."

Doctor Chang smiled. "Okay, thank you." She took the journal and turned the pages. "Ah, this is all great, Justin."

"The memories don't come back to me," he added. "No flashback or anything. They're just already there. Like Dallas' ute and the scratch on the fridge, and the old radio." He shrugged. "I just knew it."

She nodded. "That's perfectly normal."

"I just expected the mist to clear but it didn't. Nothing came to me; it was just already there."

She gave him a patient smile. "The mist?"

"Yeah, the mist. In my head. Like it's . . . hazy."

"Like everything's foggy?" I suggested.

Justin nodded. "Yeah. Foggy." He shrugged again. "Misty."

Doctor Chang read something in his journal and looked up, surprised. "Oh, the wing dream?"

Justin laughed and I felt my cheeks heat. "Yes!" he replied. "It was Dallas all along. I knew I'd remember him. Some part of him had to come back to me. I guess it was my mind's way of telling me what he meant to me."

"You have wing tattoos?" she asked. Obviously Justin had just written the word *tattoo*.

"Uh, yeah," I answered, waving my hand across my front. "Two big wings, right across my chest."

"He can show you if you want?" Justin added with a smile.

"No, I can't," I shot back, blushing even harder. *Jesus.* I gave the doc an apologetic smile, but she just chuckled.

"I believe you," she said. "And I'm happy you found the meaning of them."

"Me too," Justin replied. He gave me a shy smile that made my belly flip. "Remembering Dallas was the best thing."

My heart swelled and he smiled at me.

Doctor Chang turned another page and took a moment

to read what Justin had written. "You have some points here," she said. "Are these things you wanted to ask about?"

Justin nodded. "Yeah. I keep . . . I know there are things I should be asking. Things I should know about and worry about. I know I should. But I can't seem to get my brain to ask. It's weird. There are things I used to worry about, and I guess I still should, but I don't have the . . . room for it."

"The room for it?" I asked. "In your mind?"

"Well, yeah," he replied. "Like my head is full. Like . . ." He made a pained face, trying to find the best way to describe something. He nodded to Doctor Chang's coffee cup. "Like a cup that's full to the top. There's more to go in, but it's full already."

"Full of mist," I clarified, from what he'd told me before.

"Yeah. Everything is simple now. I can't think too hard, about anything. There's just no room."

"That's quite common," Doctor Chang said. "What you're experiencing is very normal for people who have suffered a TBI. But you want to know about these things." She tapped his journal. "And that tells me your cognitive processing is improving. Three, two, or even one week ago you wouldn't have thought to ask. And you recognise there are some issues you should be more aware of. That's a pretty big step forward."

"I know I should, but I don't know if my head can. Does that make sense?"

"Perfect sense," she replied.

"Is it something I can help with?" I asked, feeling out of the loop. I had no clue what they were talking about.

Doctor Chang replied, "Justin's noted down some things he recognises that should be important."

"Things I should know but don't."

"Such as?"

The doc read from his journal. "Money, work, rent, bills."

"I should know about that stuff, right?" Justin asked. "But I can't seem to get . . . Those are things I worried about before, in Darwin. I should worry about them now, but my head is full."

I squeezed his hand. "Well, I can answer those questions. You have your bank account and your pay from work gets deposited straight into that. We split all the utilities and bills equally between us. You pay me rent, and that goes into my mortgage. I've kept all your mail, like bank statements and all that; it's all unopened on my desk. I wasn't sure you were up for any of that. I'm sorry if that confused you."

"No. I just didn't know. I mean, I couldn't . . . my brain is full," he said. "I just kept thinking I should be worried about this stuff. Like, real-life stuff, but I couldn't seem to grasp it."

"All your bills are direct debited out of your account," I explained. "Same as mine. Phone bill, electricity instalments, that kind of thing. It's all automatic. And I've been taking care of everything else. I don't expect you to be worrying about this stuff. You need to worry about getting better, that's all."

He thought that over for a bit and frowned. "And work? My job is . . . I can't do my job."

I turned to face him better and rubbed his hand in mine. "Your job is secure. You're still getting paid even though you're not working; you're entitled to sick pay. We're waiting on workers' comp to deal with the insurance from the accident. You were driving to a job when you were hit in the van, so it should all be covered. You don't have anything to worry about. That's all being taken care of."

Even though it hadn't come through yet. It was my concern, not his. Jesus, the last thing he needed to be stressing over was money and work.

"I can show you everything when we get home," I added. "Anything you want to know."

"Are you happy with that?" the doc asked. "Is there anything else you'd like to know?"

He grimaced as he tried to think, and it was a sure sign that he was tired. Something the doc recognised as well. She closed his journal and slid it toward him. "Over the next week, I want you to write anything down you think of and we can discuss it in your next visit."

"'Kay," he said quietly. Then he sighed. "How 'm I doin', doc?"

She smiled. "You're doing great, Justin. I know it might not feel like it but you are making great progress." Then she looked at me. "Dallas, is there anything you'd like to ask?"

"Um, not that I can think of. He's been doing some jigsaw puzzles, and he's better at them than me. He's eating a little more, which is good." I smiled at him. "He'll be happier now that heavy cast on his arm is gone, though. It'll make his life easier, for sure. I think we'll have a good week."

"I think so too," she agreed. "Just get some rest this afternoon, and take it easy for a day or two."

Justin slow blinked but he was smiling. "We had our first date," he said. "Sorry, our second first date."

Doctor Chang grinned. "You did?"

"Yep. Chinese food and footy on the TV," he said, tiredly.

I grinned at him. "It was fun."

"M'heart knows him, but m'head doesn't," Justin said. "Just tryin' to catch up."

"We'll get there, Juss," I murmured.

"Sounds like you have a lot of catching up to do," she said, smiling. She spoke a little bit more about Justin's recovery, but seeing how tired he was, she boiled it right down to basically keep doing what we're doing and she'd see us again next week.

When we finally got back into my ute, he held his journal on his lap and closed his eyes.

"Wanna drive along the beach? Or just wanna go home?" I asked.

"Beach sounds good. Another day," he mumbled.

"Okay. Home it is."

He slept on the drive home, and I felt bad for waking him up when we got there. I opened his car door and gently roused him. He looked at me with bleary eyes and it took him a second to focus. He smiled. "Hey."

"Hey, beautiful," I replied. "We're home."

His grin widened and I was helping him out of the ute and onto his scooter when Sparra came over. "Got your arm out, I see," he said.

Justin glanced down at his arm in the cuff sling. "Yeah."

He always moved and spoke so much slower when he was tired, and Sparra didn't need to be told. He simply gave Juss a pat on the back. "Good to see ya, mate." Then he gave me a quick nod. "Davo wanted to see ya when you got a minute."

"Okay. I'll be right back down."

We got Justin to the bottom of the stairs but there was no way he could get himself up there. He stood up and took hold of the railing.

"Hang on," I urged. "Let me carry you."

"Carry me?"

"Yep." I slung his left arm over my shoulder and slowly picked him up, bridal style. I had to be careful of his head and his leg and his right arm. It was the only way. "Hold on."

Sparra dashed up the stairs and opened my door for me, then grinned as he came back down.

Justin chuckled and put his head on my chest. "Could get used to this."

Yeah, he was shorter than me and smaller, and he wasn't heavy at all. But carrying him up the stairs, kinda on an angle so his foot didn't catch on the railing, wasn't exactly easy. When we were inside, I gently set him down on his feet and righted myself with a groan. "Been a while since I've lifted weights or done cardio."

He smiled sleepily at me. "Was fun."

He hobbled to the couch, using his right leg as much as it would let him, and sat himself down. I got him a bottle of water while he reclined and got himself comfy. "Hey, Dall?"

I smiled at the name I hadn't heard in far too long. "Yeah?"

"Sorry 'bout the journal," he said, his eyes half-closed.

"What are you sorry for?"

"For not askin' you." His eyes drifted closed. "Just got no room for thinkin'."

I flicked the blanket out over him and planted a kiss on his forehead. "Don't be sorry," I whispered, but he was already asleep.

CHAPTER FOUR

DAVO WAS busy under an ATV when I came down into the shop. I helped him without being asked, and together we pulled out the transmission. "How's Jusso?" he asked, eventually.

"Good. Tired today. Doing too much knocks him around. He'll be asleep for a bit now. Sparra said you wanted to see me?"

"Yeah, John Simpson called. Wanted to know if we'd still be right to take on his contract. Didn't really know what to tell him. Wanted to say yes, but it's a big job and we're short-staffed."

Shit shit shit. "I know. I'll call him. I'm here for the rest of the week. Juss's got no more appointments. Sorry for dumping all this on you."

"Nah, it's okay. I just didn't want to tell him the wrong thing. I told him we were business as usual and that you'd call him back today."

"Thanks, mate. I'll go call him now."

He scratched the back of his neck, nervous. "And, uh, the order for four-stroke oil didn't go through. Something with the payment. I told them you'd call 'em back today too. We're gonna need that by Friday."

Fuck.

"Yeah, sure. I must've stuffed up the account or something. I'll sort it out, thanks. I'll go do that now. Then do ya need me to help you or Sparra? Or does something else need doing? Just tell me where we're at."

"If you wanna get started on the old Beemer. The driveshaft's had the Richard, and the swing arm on the rear is out. He thought it was a torque reaction." He rolled his eyes. "Anyway, if you could get it started, that'd be good." He cringed. "Ah, boss. Thanks."

He might have had issues with giving his boss orders, but I had no issue in taking them. "Consider it done."

A quick phone call to John Simpson sorted out that spot fire. We needed that contract and I reassured him we'd be on top of it. He said he was sorry to hear about Justin, and I could tell he was genuine, but business was business. Something I understood well.

Then to fix the next spot fire, I logged onto my bank account. Because I wasn't feeling like shit before . . .

I transferred what I could into the trading account and called the oil company to reconfirm the order, and that would have to do for now. I did a quick doublecheck of any outstanding accounts and sent them off a quick reminder to pay. No one owed us a fortune, but every dollar would help right now. I'd probably have to call the bank sooner rather than later and ask about a redraw or refinance. It wasn't something I'd ever wanted to do but maybe I didn't have much choice.

I noticed more notes on my desk with more phone messages, and with a heavy sigh, I sorted through them and made the priority calls and left the others for later.

I wanted to get that road bike up on the stand. Davo had asked specifically, and he'd really pulled through for me these last four weeks and I didn't want to let him down.

But there was another issue, which I'd tried to ignore, that probably couldn't be ignored any longer either.

We were short-staffed, and if I started to let customers down, it would be irreparable to the business. I couldn't ask any more of Davo and Sparra. I'd asked enough of them already. I needed to be the one who did this. It was my business, my responsibility. I had to work harder, faster, better, and now that Juss was home and recovering, I should be able to do just that.

I had three men depending on me. Not just Justin, but Davo and Sparra depended on me too. They needed their jobs, and Justin needed a home and a job to go back to when he was ready. I had to pull it together for them. I couldn't be losing contracts or having loyal customers feel they needed to go somewhere else.

The truth was, when I told Justin that workers' comp was taking care of everything, that wasn't exactly true. They were supposed to be, but of course, these things took time. I didn't need him worrying about that stuff. Stress could set back his recovery, and guilt was the last thing he needed.

So yeah, when I said that Justin being alive was the most important thing and everything else didn't matter, that wasn't exactly true either. Don't get me wrong; him surviving the accident was the most important thing, without question. Having him in my life was everything. But the business and clients and bills and insurance, all that mundane shit, that was kind of important too. Well, it was important now he was out of hospital and real life reared its ugly head.

Maybe Justin thinking about these real-life problems—

money, work, bills—made me realise I needed to think about them too.

So with that in mind, I got my arse out onto the floor and put a few hours in fixing an old BMW driveshaft. It was good too, using my hands, doing familiar work. It was good to switch the brain off for a bit.

I'd almost got it done when my phone beeped with a message. Juss had obviously woken up.

Where are you?

I thumbed out a quick reply. *Just downstairs. You okay?*

His reply took a few seconds. *Yeah.*

I wondered what the pause was for. Did he have a headache? Did he pause to consider telling me he wasn't okay but decided against it? *Need me to come up?*

Another pause. *No.*

I sighed, and when I looked across the shop to Davo, I found him looking at me. "I'll just be two minutes."

"No worries," he replied.

I took the stairs two at a time and found Justin getting onto his scooter. "Hey," I said. "Everything okay?"

"Yeah." He gave me a smile that, no matter how busy or distracted I was, would stop me in my tracks. "You busy down there?"

"Yeah, but it's no problem for me to come up. How's your arm?"

His arm was still in the cuff sling and he moved all his fingers. "Good. I need to pee."

I snorted. "Okay. Want me to fix you something to eat? We kinda missed lunch." I should've been more aware; he needed to eat with his meds. I went to the fridge. "Sandwich okay?"

I set about making us both a quick sandwich and put some crackers and grapes into a container for him. I got his pills and a glass of juice, and when he came back out, he downed the pills first with a long drink of juice and ate a cracker.

So no, he wasn't okay. He was in pain and hungry.

"I'm sorry. I lost track of time," I said.

"'S okay," he said. "I just woke up and you weren't here. I asked Squish where you were, but he wouldn't answer me."

I put his sandwich on the table and pulled out the seat next to him. "He can be so rude."

Justin smiled at me and took a bite of his sandwich. "Thanks for this. I should do this for you. Maybe if I set a timer on my phone . . ."

"You were exhausted. If you need to sleep, then sleep."

"It's weird," he said with a shrug. "If there's food there, I eat it. If it's not there, I don't. I don't really get hungry. I just feel sick if I don't eat but my brain doesn't tell me I'm hungry."

I think I remembered one of the docs saying something about that. How his brain might have trouble sending and receiving messages, and how hunger was one of the most common. "Then we can set an alarm on your phone," I said brightly. "If I'm stuck downstairs and you haven't eaten by one o'clock, an alarm will tell you to get yourself something. And your pills."

He frowned. "I hate that you have to do things for me."

"Hey," I whispered, reaching for his hand. "I like doing things for you. And if we have to set an alarm or something, then that's just what we have to do. It's no problem. It's just a tool we use to help us, like your scooter."

He chewed on his bottom lip and it slowly morphed into a smile. "Do you always know what to say?"

God, I could have laughed at that, because most days I

had no freaking clue. I finished chewing my sandwich and swallowed it down. "Uh, no. Actually, I don't know what I'm doing. I'm just doing my best, hoping I don't get it wrong."

His smile faded as his gaze met mine. "Don't be worried about getting anything wrong, Dallas. Your best is kinda perfect."

I pulled his hand to my lips and kissed his palm. "I gotta get back downstairs. I'm sorry, I wish I could stay here with you. But I just need a few more hours, then I'll be back."

"'S okay," he said. "I feel better now, but I'm still beat. I'll be having another nap, I think."

"Can I get you anything before I go?"

"Nah, I'm good."

I stood up and took my plate to the sink. God, I wished I didn't have to leave him right now. I looked at the door and sighed.

"Dallas?"

"Yeah?"

Justin got off his scooter and stood up slowly. "There is something you can get me."

"What's that?"

"A hug. I need a hug."

Christ, I could have cried. I threw my arms around him and held him, breathing him in, his scent, his warmth, the feel of him against me. I didn't want to let go. Not now, not ever. "I needed this too," I whispered.

He rubbed my back with his good arm and buried his face in my neck, and for a long, perfect moment, we never moved. All my worries stripped away; everything that plagued me just minutes earlier was gone. This was what mattered. Justin was what mattered most.

"One more thing," he said.

I pulled back so I could see his face. "Sure."

He pointed to his mouth. "Kiss me?"

Smiling, I took hold of his face and watched as he gasped, his eyes fluttering closed. I brought his chin up and caressed his lips with mine, ghosting a kiss before kissing him deeper. I gave him the barest of tongue, the sweetest taste, before pulling away. His eyes were still closed and when he opened them, he looked drunk. It took him an adorable second to focus on me.

"Oh," he breathed.

I laughed. "You 'right to stand by yourself?"

He chuckled and sank his teeth into his bottom lip. His cheeks were pink, his eyes had stars. "Wow."

"Here, let me get your scooter," I said, helping him sit on it. "You okay?"

"Mm," he replied. "Much better."

"Me too," I said. I put my finger under his chin and leaned down to peck his lips again. "I won't be long."

He gave me a lazy smirk as I walked out. I took the stairs with a skip in my step. Davo spotted me. "Is Jusso all right?"

I was certainly happier now than I was when I dashed up the stairs earlier. "Sure. Just a bit of a reality check, that's all."

He cocked his head. "Reality check?"

Yes, reality. Both the business and Justin needed me equally. I needed to do more, be more. "Yep. Now, what else did you need me to do?"

DAVO AND SPARRA left at knock-off time and I stuck around to get as much done as I could. I did some maths before putting in a few stock orders, making sure I had enough in my account this time. I hated that I needed to be so cautious, that I had to count every cent and transfer money between accounts so I could pay bills. It was a stress I just didn't need.

I returned some phone calls, tidied up, and swept the whole shop out. I got everything ready for the morning, locked up, took all the papers from my desk and my laptop, and went upstairs.

Juss was asleep on the couch when I walked in, Squish purring loudly on his lap. The TV was on some animal documentary and I smiled at the thought of Juss putting something on for Squish to watch. The photographs I'd given him at the hospital were on the couch beside him, with his journal and his phone, and the jigsaw on the table was almost complete, so he'd had a busy afternoon.

He stirred when I put my stuff down. "Hey, didn't mean to wake you," I said quietly.

"Just dozing," he replied, sitting up. "What time is it?"

"Almost six."

"Was gonna cook dinner," he said. He sat the recliner up, then lifted Squish off his lap so he could stand. "Got the meat out of the freezer."

"You want to cook?" I asked, surprised.

"Yeah." He frowned. "Is that okay?"

"Absolutely!" I said, grinning.

Happier now, he got on his scooter and went to the cupboard by the stove. "I want to do stuff. Help out, ya know?"

"I have some paperwork to get through, so you cooking dinner would be incredibly helpful, thank you."

He beamed. "Well, I dunno how good it'll be. If it's awful, we might be having toast."

"What are you gonna cook?"

"My nan's spaghetti. I remember how to cook it, so . . ."

"Was always a favourite of mine." He used to cook it often, and I was oddly glad that his nan had passed away before he moved to Darwin. He remembered she was gone, and I couldn't bear the thought of him having to grieve a second time. I squeezed his shoulder on my way to the fridge. "Can I get the chef a drink? Orange and mango mineral water, plain water, juice?"

"Um . . . A mineral water, thanks. Sick of plain water today."

Truth be told, I didn't get much work done. He needed help lifting stuff, but it didn't matter. Helping him reclaim some independence was important. I didn't do any of the cooking part; that was all him. But he couldn't fill the pot and carry it to the stove with one arm whilst on a scooter.

And when I wasn't helping, I was watching. It was good to see him doing things, even mundane things like cooking. Especially mundane, everyday things, even though I had to remind myself this was far from mundane for Justin. The fact he wanted to help out, and even that he thought to help out, was a pretty big deal.

"You keep staring at me," he said. He was now standing by the stove, stirring the pot. The smell in the flat was amazing, and seeing him concentrate and taste, adding a bit of this and a touch of that, and stirring some more just made me so damn happy.

"Because you're kinda great, you know that?"

He made a face and shook his head, as though it was too absurd to be true, but then he shot me a strange look. Startled and confused? He put his hand to his head. "Oh."

"Oh, what?" I said, getting to my feet. If he felt dizzy, should he be about to fall . . .

"I . . . I think I remember something," he mumbled. He

frowned again. "Did we . . . ? Did I . . . ? I made this for you before." He looked around the kitchen as though something didn't make sense. "But not here. The kitchen was yellow."

I took a step toward him. "You remember that?"

"Did that happen?"

"Yes! At your old flat. Where you lived at when you moved back to Newcastle from Darwin. The flat was tiny and the kitchen was just one small bank of cupboards with a sink. The walls were yellow."

"I remember," he said. "I had a flashback. Of me cooking. I can't see you but I know I'm cooking for you, and I was nervous but you said it smelled great and then I said . . . something. And you said, 'Because you're kinda great, you know that?' just like you said now." He stared at me, his eyes wide. "Oh my God, I remember that."

I went to him and put my hands on his shoulders, his neck, his jaw, and I pulled him in for a hug. I was surprised by how emotional it made me. But he remembered something else, something to do with me, with us.

"You asked me to your place for dinner. You were so nervous," I told him. "But dinner was amazing. You had an old table with three mismatched chairs and a couch you'd bought second hand. We watched a movie on TV. Um, *Beverly Hills Cop*, I think."

He laughed into my neck, but it was teary. "That's something I'd watch."

I pulled back and slid my hand along his jaw. I stared into those dark brown eyes and thumbed his cheek. "You remembered something."

He nodded, still teary. "Must have been what you said and me cooking the same food. I don't know. But it came back to me."

I rested my forehead to his. "I'm so happy for you."

He closed his eyes. "It's just another random thing, though. Nothing too important."

"Are you kidding, baby? That's huge and very important!"

He sighed and one corner of his mouth lifted. "I like it when you call me baby."

That made me smile. "Anything you remember is important," I said. "Every single thing."

"I wish I could see your face," he said sadly. "In my memory. I can hear your laugh, though. And I know it's you. I can feel it."

I lifted his chin and pecked his lips. "Baby, that's amazing."

He rested his head on my shoulder and looked at the stove. "Shit, I'm burning dinner."

I laughed and we turned everything off and I drained the spaghetti and he plated it up. We sat at the table and he waited for me to take the first taste.

"Oh, this is good," I said with my mouth half-full. "Just like you always make it."

He took a small bite and gave it an approving nod. "It's not bad."

We ate in silence for a few bites, and I paused to take a sip of my drink. I tapped my can to his. "Compliments to the chef."

He was happier, and if that was because he'd cooked dinner or because he remembered something or because he liked my compliment, I wasn't sure. Maybe it was all three.

"Did you say accounts?" he asked, nodding toward where I'd stacked the papers on top of my laptop.

I wasn't gonna tell him about my money worries, but I didn't want to hide this from him. Maybe just not the extent of it. It was a fine line. "Yeah. I just have a few things to get done tonight. I'll need to be working in the shop with the boys this week and not in the office, so if I can keep on top of the paperwork . . ."

"Is that because I'm not there?" he asked. "Do you have to do my job?"

Shit. I withheld the sigh that threatened to escape and put my fork down. "Not exactly. I mean, yes, a little bit. But it's nothing we can't handle until you're ready to come back."

His brow furrowed and I gave him time to think about what I'd said. He ate some more of his pasta but then pushed what was left around his plate with his fork. "Do Davo and Sparra have to do my work too?"

Shit.

I didn't want him to feel bad, but I also wouldn't lie to him. "The three of us are filling in the gaps. When I was at the hospital every day, Davo and Sparra did everything. They really covered my arse. So now we're home, I'm trying to do as much as I can to help them out. We have an important contract coming up, one we do every year, and it's good money. I can't drop the ball on it."

"I don't like letting you down," he whispered.

I reached over and squeezed his arm. "You're not. At all. In any way. You're my priority, first and foremost, Jussy. But my business is important too. Davo and Sparra depend on me for a job and I don't want to let them down. I just need to get the balance right, that's all. So if I have to do some work on the computer while we sit on the couch after dinner, then so be it."

He tried to smile but couldn't quite manage it. "My accident . . ."

When he said nothing else, I did. "Your accident was not your fault. It wasn't anyone's fault. And we'll get through this, I have no doubt. I just want to try and do the right thing by everyone, that's all."

"I want to help. I can do . . ." He frowned again, like he couldn't find the right word. He shrugged. "I don't know what I can do."

"You can get better, and you can rest and recover," I said. "And you can make an awesome spaghetti."

That earned me a small smile, but it didn't last long. "I hate that everything is so hard. I want to do things but I'm tired, and my leg and my arm are stupid, and my head hurts most of the time. And the worst part is that I can't think properly. Like sometimes it's clear, and sometimes it's foggy, sometimes it's like I'm underwater. I hate that I can't remember everything, and I hate that I feel so lost."

"Lost?"

He gave a small nod. "I dunno who I am. I mean, I know I'm Justin, and I know where I come from, and all that shit. But I dunno who I was. The last five years were so important and I've lost that. I dunno who *that* Justin is."

I pulled my chair around so I faced him, and I took his hand. "Baby, I wish I could fix that. I wish I knew how to get everything back. I hate that you feel that way, but I completely understand why you do. I'm sure I'd feel the same if it were me in that van that day."

"I just feel . . . lost. And sad." He shrugged. "I guess today's just a bad day, but I . . ." His chin wobbled and his eyes became glassy. "I dunno."

"Oh, baby," I whispered. "You're allowed to have bad days." To be honest, I was surprised he hadn't had more bad days before now. "Do you want a hug?"

He nodded quickly, and I stood up and helped him to his feet. I pulled him against me and he snuggled in, fitting the side of his head against my neck. I rubbed his back and held him tight, and for the longest moment, we never moved.

"Thank you," he mumbled.

"What are you thanking me for?"

"For everything. For knowing what I need when I don't."

He made no attempt to move and I certainly wasn't going to. "I need your hugs too."

"I mean it. When I'm all fuzzy and . . . not together . . . I can't think of the word. Anyway, when I'm like that, you hug me and it fixes me."

"Well, you're welcome. You can have a hug any time."

He was quiet again for a bit and he leaned heavily against me as though he were falling asleep. "Thank you for staying."

"Staying where?" *In this hug?*

"With me. For not leaving me. You could have, but you didn't."

I pulled back then so he could see the seriousness in my eyes. "Justin, baby. I love you. I've loved you for years. You are loved. And I know that's probably weird for you, but I need you to know this: I'm not leaving you. Not then, not now, not ever."

His face softened and he almost smiled. "It's not weird. Well, maybe a little bit but not really. We've been on like, one date."

I laughed. "Does tonight not count? You cooked me dinner. It could be our second date."

"Nope. I forgot the candles."

I chuckled and pulled him back in for a hug. His left arm went around me and held me just as tight as I held him. He was warm and smelled like home. "Candles make it a date," I said quietly. "Got it."

He was quiet again and heavy against me. "I like hearing you say it," he mumbled. "That you love me. I know you do. You look after me, and you care."

He liked knowing he was loved, and I couldn't blame him. It was an amazing feeling, comforting like a soft bed and warm blankets on a cold night. I knew he loved me too. I *knew* he did. It was just trapped, hidden under the surface. He'd already remembered slivers of me from our life before the accident. He said my wing tattoos felt safe, like home. And he trusted me, and for a guy who was surrounded by strangers, that was a helluva statement.

His heart knew me, even if his head didn't.

And I clung to that with everything I had.

"Tired," he mumbled.

"Let's get you into bed," I said, leaving his arms to get his scooter.

He took his meds, brushed his teeth, and I helped him into bed. He was too tired for anything else tonight, and I reasoned he'd feel better in the morning after a shower. Squish followed him onto the bed and I sat on the edge of the bed beside Juss. He was smiling as he drifted off and I kissed his forehead before I left them to sleep.

I cleaned up after dinner—Justin had never been a tidy cook—then sat at the table and fired up my laptop. I managed to put a dent in my paperwork, paying what bills I could afford and watching my bank overdraft with every invoice, but after a while, I could barely keep my eyes open.

I turned everything off and used the bathroom, then stood in the hall wondering which bed I should sleep in. My head told me to go to my room, but my heart was across the hall in our old bed . . .

I didn't get to make that decision, though. Because Juss

started to stir and fuss in his sleep, and as I got to the door, he startled awake, sitting up with a gasp and a cry. "Dallas?"

I went straight to him. "Hey, baby. I'm right here."

He clung to me, pawing at my arm and my hand. "Sleep here. Need you here with me."

"Okay," I whispered. I crawled over him and got under the covers. He was snuggled into my side before my head was even on the pillow. "You okay now?"

He murmured something affirmative and sighed, slipping straight back to sleep. I wrapped him in my arms and inhaled deeply. It was so familiar and lovely, but a little strange. Our relationship was now unusual and complicated, to say the least. I knew everything about him, but he was just beginning to know me. We'd been together for years but were technically dating again, we'd made love hundreds of times, but to him, we'd only kissed a handful of times. Four weeks ago, he had no clue who I was, yet he couldn't sleep without me.

So yeah, it was weird and complicated, but it was kind of wonderful too.

We got a second chance, and not everyone did. I wasn't about to waste that. Sure, I had to juggle work and a business and clients and staff. I never expected this to be easy, and honestly, I reckoned we got out of it easier than those in a lot of the stories I'd read about brain injury.

I just had to count my blessings and take each day as it came.

Was getting to hold Juss while he slept a blessing? Hell fucking yes it was.

I WOKE up when Justin rolled over. He slept soundly.

Clearly having the cast off his arm was more comfortable for him. He sure was peaceful.

I got out of bed before him because I was only wearing boxer briefs and I didn't want my morning wood to make things awkward. A shower and a quick wank took care of the wood issue. I got dressed and began making breakfast.

Justin came out on his scooter, scowling, still half-asleep. His grumpy morning face always made me smile. "Coffee?" I asked.

"Hmm."

"Toast?"

"Hmm."

I chuckled as I handed him a piece of toast. "Butter and Vegemite," I said as I went to the fridge for the milk.

He even chewed grumpily. "You're happy this morning?"

"Yep." I grinned at him and put his coffee on the kitchen counter. This was our morning routine now. Same as the day before, and the day before that. It wasn't monotonous to me. It was establishing familiarity for Juss, someone with a brain injury, something he could depend on. "Sleep okay?"

He frowned. "Can only sleep if you're there, apparently."

"I don't mind. I sleep better when I sleep with you too."

He sipped his decaf coffee and his scowl lessened a little. "Need a shower."

"Okay," I said easily. "What are your plans for the day?"

His angry brow returned. "Couch. TV. Jigsaw puzzle. Boring shit. Nap, followed by more boring shit."

"How d'ya feel today? Okay?"

"Better. Not as tired as I thought I'd be."

"Your home-care nurse will be here at nine."

He sighed and drank more coffee, and I began to wonder if there was more to his demeanour than just being his old not-a-morning person. He seemed more sad than grumpy.

I waited for him to get out of the shower, tidying up and wiping everything down. I packed up my laptop and all my papers from last night and was pulling my boots on when he came out. He walked, limping on his injured leg and pushing his scooter, to the couch. He was wearing a pair of shorts and one of my old T-shirts that looked really good on him. He offered half a smile, but it wasn't very happy.

"How does your arm feel out of the cast?" I asked. "Good to finally be able to wet and wash it?"

"Yeah," he said. He opened and closed his fist and wiggled his fingers. He straightened his elbow a bit and turned his palm upward, but not all the way. "Doesn't like to move much, but it's better."

When he was on the couch, I put a bottle of water beside him and planted a kiss on the top of his freshly washed hair. "I'll be downstairs. Call or text me if you need me."

"Hmm" was his only reply.

Yeah, he was definitely sad and cranky today. I left him to it and went downstairs, opening up the shop, trying to get a head start before the boys arrived. Before I knew it, they rolled in and work began. And I swear, just a few minutes later, Justin's nurse, Megan, arrived.

I needed more hours in the day.

I met Megan at the bottom of the stairs. "Just a sec," I said quietly, wiping my hands on my work pants.

"Everything okay?" she asked.

"Yeah, he was just a bit out of sorts this morning. He's never been a morning person, but he seems . . . sad." I didn't want to say depressed because I certainly couldn't diagnose that. "Just wanted to give you a heads up."

"Thanks. I appreciate it."

"Let me know if there's something he needs," I added. "He might be more comfortable telling you? I don't know . . . He said last night he worried that he was a burden, basically. Not working, not contributing, that kind of thing. I told him the only thing he needs to do is get better, but I don't think that helped much."

She patted my arm and smiled. "I'll go check on him."

I watched her go up the stairs and when I looked back into the shop, I saw Sparra watching me. "Everything all right, boss?"

"Yeah, mate. Jusso was a bit down last night and this morning. I just wanted to give the nurse a heads up, that's all."

Sparra frowned. "Is he all right?"

"Yeah. Just part of the process, apparently. He's okay. I'll wait to see what Megan says after she sees him."

"Has to be hard on him. He must feel like a stranger," Sparra said. "Let me know if there's anything I can do."

"I will, thanks," I said, clapping him on the shoulder before we went back to our work. I went back to the bike I'd been working on and tried to keep myself occupied, which wasn't entirely easy with one eye on the back stairs. And I couldn't help but think of something Justin said last night and what Sparra had said earlier.

After an eternity, which was probably closer to thirty minutes, Megan appeared. I left my station and she smiled as I walked over. "How is he?"

She gave a serious nod. "Yeah, he's okay. Like you said, he's feeling pretty low. It's not uncommon. But his arm looks good, his range of motion is good. He's walking more, his meds are all fine."

"He remembered something yesterday," I said. "Like an actual memory. Everything else has been kind of factual, but this was a memory."

Megan smiled. "He told me that."

"Hey, can I ask you something?" Then I added quickly, "It's about Justin."

"Sure. You can ask; what I can answer is a different story."

"Yeah, that's fine, it's just that . . . He said he was feeling kinda lost and even bored, I guess. Everything feels so strange to him, which is understandable. But what if he came down here into the workshop for an hour or two every day? Maybe just in the mornings, when he's not so tired. Not to work or anything, but just to be . . . included."

Megan smiled. "I think he'd like that."

I know he'd like it. "Yeah, but is he up for that? Is it too soon? I don't want to rush him if he's not ready. And what if he gets hurt?"

"I think he's up for it. But maybe start with a short time first up," she suggested. "It might help him reconnect with who he is. It's very common for someone with amnesia to feel disconnected with who they were before and who they are now."

"He's a mechanic," I said. "One of the best motocross bike mechanics in town."

"Then, sure," she replied. "Let him try. Just remember, he tires easily. Nothing strenuous, nothing heavy or fast. He'll need to readjust to how his brain receives and responds. His reaction times are much slower."

"Yeah, of course."

She said she'd be back tomorrow, though I didn't even

wait for her to get halfway to her car before I raced up the stairs and into the flat. Justin was at the table, staring at the jigsaw puzzle. "Hey," I said. "How was your session with Megan?"

He shrugged, then sighed. "Okay."

"How's the puzzle going?" I asked.

"It's shit." He'd almost finished it, but clearly, he wasn't happy with it. "This isn't my idea of fun."

I went and sat beside him. "I know, baby."

He chewed on the inside of his lip, not making eye contact with me. "I just . . . I know I have a long road ahead of me. But I'm starting to think I'll never be back to who I was."

"What if I suggested something that might help?" I asked. "If you're feeling up to it, that is."

"I don't want to do any more fucking puzzles, Dallas."

I took his hand. "What about a different kind of puzzle? One you love and could probably do with your eyes closed."

His gaze met mine, interest piqued.

"It would mean coming downstairs for a bit. Like maybe an hour or so every morning."

"A puzzle?" he asked with the barest hint of a smile. "Downstairs?"

"Yep." I stood up. "Come on, on your feet."

He smiled now and slowly stood. "Okay . . . ?"

"I'll take your scooter down the stairs," I said, picking it up and running it to the bottom of the stairs. When I got back up to the top, Juss was at the door. "Okay, you ready?"

He nodded and we came down the stairs like we did the other day. Him, slowly, one step at a time, and me, in front and facing him, going down backwards so I could hold him. I helped him onto the scooter, and when we went into the workshop, he was smiling.

"Here's the big fella," Davo said, spotting him, grinning. "Has he got you working already?"

"Not sure," he replied. "Some kind of puzzle."

Davo nodded, knowingly. "Ah, great idea."

"It was Davo's idea," I admitted. "And then Sparra said something earlier about how you being upstairs must make you feel like a stranger, and I realised he was right. You need to be included, down here where you belong. With us. Doing what you love."

Justin's eyes met mine and his smile softened. "Thanks."

"You're welcome. The puzzle, though," I said, waving my hand to the back corner. "Two Kawasaki two-stroke engine blocks that need to be pulled apart and cleaned, moving parts replaced, and all put back together again."

The truth was, this was a menial task. Pain-in-the-arse jobs we'd put off forever, but they could be perfect for Justin. No brain splitting thinking required, just procedural motions. Sparra's jigsaw puzzles had been a great idea, but Davo's real-life motorbike engine puzzle idea was even better.

Justin stared at me, disbelievingly. "You want me to do that?"

"You reckon you're up for it?"

His smile morphed into a grin. "Hell yes." But then he got a little teary. He swallowed hard and took a deep breath. "Thank you."

I stepped in closer and put my arm around him. "You're very welcome."

CHAPTER FIVE

DAVO LOWERED the movable workbench and locked the wheels down tight, giving Justin a workstation which was more suitable to his scooter. I carried the first engine over for him but left him to find all his tools and equipment. It was part of the process, after all: getting him back on the team and keeping him busy and productive.

I kept an eye on him, and even with his right arm still in the collar-cuff, he never stopped smiling.

Even when he became tired just before lunch, he really was so much happier.

He found everything he needed: he sometimes walked to it, sometimes scooted over to get whichever tool he needed. But his smile . . .

It was so worth it.

When his blinks began to get longer, I went over. "How're you going with it?"

"Good," he said, looking up at me. He was happy but oh so tired. "Got lots done."

It was true. He was making great progress. "It's almost lunchtime," I said. "And you look beat."

He gave a small nod. "Wish I wasn't tired."

"I know. But the best part is that you can do this again tomorrow."

"Tomorrow?"

"Yeah. Nurse Megan said you should only do a few hours each morning. Just to start with." Okay, so that wasn't entirely true, but a medical professional's opinion held more water than mine. She had suggested just a few hours, but it was really me who didn't want him to overdo it. Plus, I was pretty sure once he got himself onto the couch, he was gonna nap for a good while.

"Okay," he murmured. "I can finish this off tomorrow, right?"

"Sure you can. If you want to."

He smiled again. "I want to."

"Come on, let's get you upstairs." We went to the bottom step but there was no way he was gonna make that climb, not with how tired he was. He stood up off his scooter and held the handrail. "Hey baby," I whispered. "Put your arm around my neck. I'll carry you."

He shot me a humoured look. "Only 'cause you called me baby."

I picked him up bridal style, careful of his leg and arm, and carried him up. I got him inside, and when I lowered his feet to the floor, he kept his arm around my neck. We were incredibly close, our faces barely an inch apart. His eyes went to my mouth, then to my eyes.

I knew that look . . .

"Kiss me," he murmured.

I brought our lips together, but it was he who deepened the kiss. Like someone flipped a switch and he suddenly remembered that kissing was a thing, he tilted his head and opened his mouth for my tongue. I slid my arms around him, pulling our bodies flush, every cell in my body alight.

He groaned and felt heavy in my arms. He was tired, and his kisses were like the sleepy Sunday morning kisses we'd shared so many times. I broke the kiss and he smiled before letting his head fall to my chest.

"Okay, sleeping beauty," I said. "Let's get you onto the couch."

I helped him sit and he reclined his seat, closing his eyes already. "Tired."

I gently brushed my fingers through the hair at his temple. "Go to sleep. I'll put your lunch beside you for when you wake up."

"Hmm," he murmured, but was already out.

I studied his sleeping face; the small scar above his eye, the huge scar down the side of his head. The way his dark lashes fanned out, his stubble, how his lips were wet from our kiss, smiling . . .

God, he was beautiful.

I made him some cheese sandwiches and put them in a Squish-proof container, along with a bottle of water and a banana, and set them beside him. He stirred awake. "Sorry, baby. Didn't mean to wake you. Here's your lunch."

Bleary-eyed and barely awake, he ate half a sandwich and downed half the water and was already snoring softly by the time I put my plate in the sink. Certain now that he'd eaten something, he'd sleep for a while, I went back to work.

"He seemed happier," Sparra said as I walked in.

"So much happier," I replied, though I was sure he and Davo could tell by my smile.

"Is he resting okay now?" Davo asked.

"He's snoring already. So I reckon I've got about three hours before he wakes up and I get a text from him." I checked my watch. "Let's see how much I can get done before then."

Davo laughed, but I did get a lot done. I was also right about getting a text message from Jussy as soon as he woke up.

Thanks for the sandwiches

I grinned at my phone. *You're welcome*

Did you kiss me?

I stared at my phone, wondering what the hell that was about when he sent through another.

Or was I dreaming?

Now I laughed. *You weren't dreaming. You asked me to kiss you*

His reply took a little while. *Was thinking . . . maybe second date tonight?*

I replied immediately. *Yes please*

Second second date. With candles

Yes, I typed out. *Our second second date. What did you want to do?*

More kissing

I barked out a laugh, the sound echoing through the workshop. *Yes please*

There was nothing for a few moments and I wondered if that was the end of it. Then my phone beeped again. *Dallas?*

Yeah?

I think I really like you

I laughed again, and so God help me, I wanted to hug my phone. *I think I really like you too*

I looked up to find Davo smiling at me. He shook his head. "Just like how you were in the old days."

"What old days?"

"When you two first started out. That's how you used to look at your phone all the time."

I rolled my eyes. "Did not."

He snorted. "When he's down here tomorrow, need me to lock you both in your office again? I'll do it. Just say the word."

I smirked. "Nah, thanks. I think we're good."

He nodded, smiling. "Glad to hear. Now can you help me get these bearings out?"

"Yeah, of course." I really liked working with Davo. We'd worked together for a lot of years, since I was nineteen, actually. He was a champion bloke and had become my closest friend—outside Justin, that is. We didn't need to talk when we worked. We just got it done, each knowing what we had to do without saying.

It made time go quicker, and we were twice as productive. It was a good distraction too. I only thought about Justin maybe fifty times instead of a hundred. Yes, it was great to get work done, but I was grateful when knock-off time rolled around.

Same as the day before, when I locked everything up, I took some paperwork upstairs with me. The TV was on, volume low, but there was no Justin and his scooter was beside the couch. I was just about to call out when I heard the toilet flush and then the water at the bathroom sink.

I put my laptop down on the table just as Justin walked out. Well, it was a limp, but he was still walking. "Hey. I thought I heard the roller door close," he said with a smile.

The fact he heard anything from downstairs was kind of new. His brain registering new and different things was a good sign.

"Hi," I replied. "You look good."

"Oh," he looked down at his clothes. "Um, thanks? I don't know who owns this shirt."

I laughed. "Sorry, I meant you looked good, up and walking around and happy."

He walked over to stand a foot in front of me. "Leg feels pretty good, though I had a decent sleep at lunch. I'm always better after a good sleep. And me and Squish spent the afternoon resting pretty easy."

I noticed then, a little late, that he wasn't wearing his collar-cuff thing. "How's your arm feel?"

"Yeah, all right. That sling thing was pissing me off. I took it off not long ago." He slowly straightened his arm, proving his point that his arm was fine.

"Good, I'm glad," I said. "Must feel good to be on your feet again and to have your arm back."

"Hell yes."

"And the shirt was mine, originally," I said. "But we usually just wear whatever's clean. Our wardrobe merged a long time ago."

He looked down at the Rip Curl shirt. "Thought it was too big for me, but I still like it. Or maybe I like it because it's yours."

That sent a bloom of warmth through my chest. "So what were you thinking we should do for our second, second date?"

"Dunno. It's probably gonna be something boring like dinner and maybe that TV show you mentioned, which I'll probably fall asleep trying to watch." He made a face. "Is that lame? You probably want to do something like going out or—"

"Are you kidding? That sounds perfect to me."

He took a small step closer and took my hand. He

seemed suddenly nervous, blinking and licking his lips. "I want to thank you for today."

Oh, baby. "You don't need to thank me. You seemed so sad, like you needed to do something you used to do. You needed to do something familiar and something that reminded you of who you are."

"I did. But I didn't know that was what I needed. I just felt all wrong and useless, but I didn't know how to say that. But you knew what I needed."

"Because I know you, Juss." I gently skimmed my fingers from the hair at his forehead and down to his jaw. "I know the old Justin needed to be working and pulling bikes apart, and fixing them is what you know. It's what you do, what you've always done. The new you isn't much different at all."

"Sometimes I don't think I know who I am," he whispered. "But you do."

"You're still the same, Juss. We just need to help you reconnect with that, that's all."

He sighed. "I don't know where I'd be without you."

I took his face in my hands and kissed his forehead, his cheekbone, his lips. "You're gonna be okay, baby. We got this. You and me."

He leaned into me and his arms went around me, and for a long moment, we just stood there holding each other. Until my dick started to get ideas . . .

Needing to put some space between us, I pulled back. "Okay, so let's make a start on dinner." I went to the fridge and pulled out some minced meat. "How about rissoles and gravy and some mash."

He gave me a lazy smile. "Perfect."

There was something else in his eyes, something warm and kind that glittered with familiarity. It was how he used to look at me. I tried not to read too much into it or to get ahead of myself, but it was hard to ignore the flood of butterflies in my belly.

I began making the rissoles and Justin peeled the potatoes, and being side by side with him at the kitchen sink felt kind of surreal.

"What are you smiling at?" he asked.

I chuckled and gently nudged him with my shoulder. "Nothing. Just happy."

He grinned at that. "Me too. I'm already looking forward to tomorrow."

That made my heart soar. Giving him the smallest, mundane job had impacted him so much. He was finally beginning to feel like himself again, even if for just a few hours a day. "Me too."

After we'd eaten and cleaned up, we ventured to the couch. And just like always, I sat next to him and he automatically moved closer and snuggled in. But this time, instead of putting the footrests up, we ended up lying down, with my head on the armrest and him at the front as the little spoon. We turned the TV on, but Justin rolled over to face me, careful of his arm and leg.

He was smiling and peaceful and a little dozy. "Hey, Dall, tell me what we did on our first holiday. Where did we go? Did we even go somewhere?"

I trailed my fingers through his hair. "Just for long weekends, usually," I murmured. "I couldn't really leave the shop for long, maybe just a day or two. First time we went away together was just up the coast to Hallidays Point."

"Did we stay on the beach?"

"Yep, but it was freezing cold," I said, smiling at the memory.

"Did we take our bikes?"

"Sure did. We put them in the back of the ute and drove up, but we rode our bikes along the trails in the national park up there."

The corner of his mouth pulled upward. "Sounds like something I'd do."

I chuckled. "It was a great weekend."

"But it was cold? Why'd we go to the beach in winter?"

"It was some winter escape deal you saw in the paper."

"Did we go swimming?"

"We, uh . . . No, we didn't venture out too much. Just to ride our bikes."

He slow blinked and gave a lazy smile. He didn't seem to cotton on to the reason why we didn't venture out too much. Because we basically spent the entire weekend in bed, save two rides on the bike trails. But now, with him lying so close and me thinking back to that weekend, my dick started paying attention.

I shuffled my hips back a little as much as the couch would allow, though he was oblivious to my growing erection.

"Hey, when's your birthday?" he asked.

I grinned. "July thirtieth."

He met my gaze. "Winter. Did we go away for your birthday?"

"Yes. It was your idea. You surprised me with a weekend away."

He chuckled. "That was nice of me."

That made me laugh. "It sure was." I studied his eyes for a long moment. "We can do that again one day. A weekend at the beach or in the country somewhere. When you're feeling up for it."

He sighed. "I just want to get back to work. That sounds weird, probably. But . . ."

"But what?"

"But I know work. You showed me that today. I know how to pull engines apart, like how I know how to get dressed, or how to walk. It's just like you said: it's what I am, it's what I do." His mouth drew downward. "Since the accident, there hasn't been much that I really know. Losing five years of my life has been shit, and there's been so much that I've had to relearn. But I know bikes."

I thumbed his eyebrow. "You sure do. And baby, if you wanna work, then we work. I don't mind one bit. I have some catching up to do."

"And I want to help."

"You will. Tomorrow morning, for a few hours until Megan turns up, you're back on duty."

That earned me my favourite grin again, but his eyes closed and I thought he might fall asleep. "I like being here, like this, with you."

I stroked his cheek again, taking in every aspect of his beautiful face. "I like it too."

"Tired again," he mumbled.

"We should get you into bed. I'm kind of pinned-in here. Gonna need you to get up first."

He didn't open his eyes when he mumbled, "You make me sleepy. Warm and safe."

I could have kissed him, and I almost did. But he was half-asleep and that would've felt wrong. "C'mon, baby. Time to get up."

He cracked one eye, then the other, and after a bit more rousing, he finally got up. We got ready for bed and I turned everything off with every intention of going back out to the table to do some paperwork while he slept. But I helped him into bed, and he kept a hold of my hand, so I had a choice: I could leave him and get my work finished, or I could crawl into bed with him and relish the feel of him in my arms.

It was never a contest.

And he never stirred with a nightmare, because he clung to me like a magnet and I never let him go. He slept right through until morning when he woke up with a start.

He sat up in bed, scowling his usual grumpy morning glare at me. He rubbed the scar down the side of his head, and his right eye closed before the left and he squinted like he had a headache. Then he yawned and looked around the room, then at me. "Oh."

"Oh, what?" He sounded disappointed when he saw it was me he was in bed with. "You okay?"

"Yeah. Just a stupid dream. Remember that time we went to your Aunt Robyn's seventieth birthday and she made that lime jelly cake with coconut, and it was the grossest shit ever? I dreamed about eating that." He shook his head slowly. "Fucking weird."

I stared at him and sat up because he didn't even realise . . .

"Justin, you just remembered something."

"Yeah, it was—" His eyes went wide, his jaw slack. "Holy shit."

I barked out a laugh. "But you're right. That cake was the grossest shit ever."

He laughed too, disbelieving. "I remember it. A stupid cake, of all things." He screwed his face up and shook his head. "I dreamed it, but now I remember it! You were there! You wore that chequered blue shirt and you were laughing at something . . ."

"Probably the cake," I said. "But oh my God. You remembered something! And you can remember the shirt I wore?"

"Yes! When was that?"

"Uh, like three years ago."

He broke out in a grin. "I remember something. Something with you in it! And remember, you wanted to leave early but your brother got really drunk, so then you wanted to stick around to see him make a tit of himself."

I burst out laughing. "Yes!" I gave him a side-on hug. "Baby, you remembered something!"

He stared at me, his expression full of awe. "And we had to call into the supermarket on the way and get some flowers because your dad asked us to. And your cousin had to drive your brother home because he was so drunk and he spewed in his car, and you laughed for two days. And the next week we had that delivery fuck-up with the spare parts. Remember? They sent us the wrong order. And we tried that new pizza place. And holy fuck, Dallas, I can remember this." He became teary and his chin wobbled. "I remember it. I was there. I can actually remember and what it felt like . . . I can remember that week, or parts of it, at least. What does that mean?"

I rubbed his back. "I don't know, baby. But it's a good thing. Can you think of anything else?"

He squinted a bit, then shook his head. "I dunno. Maybe. Not really. It's just there, snippets and pieces, like it was never gone."

I leaned down and kissed his bare shoulder. "That's so awesome."

He laughed. "We tried that new pizza place and it was too fancy for us. Who the fuck puts rocket and feta on a pizza? But we tried the meat lovers and you reckoned it tasted like goat." He covered his grin with his hand; his eyes became glassy. "Dallas, I remember! I remember you."

Then he took a deep breath and nodded and began to cry.

"Oh, baby. It's okay," I whispered, pulling him down onto the bed so I could hold him properly. "It's okay."

He cried and sobbed into my chest and I held him as tight as I could. "I remember you," he mumbled. "It was all I wanted, to remember you, your face, your smile. I felt like I was letting you down because I couldn't remember . . ."

I rubbed his back and kissed the side of his head. "You could never let me down. I love you, Justin, whether you remember me or not."

He pulled back a little and, taking my hand, put my palm to his chest. "I felt those memories in here." He kept his face down so I couldn't see his eyes. "That connection. I felt it, in my memories. In here." He looked up then. "What we have is real."

I laughed and kinda cried at the same time. I was so freaking happy and relieved and floored. All my emotions were scrambled. "It's real, Juss. It's the realest thing I've ever known."

He sighed and put his head back to my chest. "These wings," he said, putting his hand to my tattoo. "I knew these wings and how they felt like home. But these memories are different, somehow. And there was a yellow Charger. Who drove a yellow Charger?"

"Sparra owned a yellow Charger," I answered. "But that was years before my Aunt's birthday and awful cake."

"It had a black stripe up the side."

"Yes, that's right."

"And you gave me my KTM . . ." He shot back and stared at me. "You gave it to me as a birthday present. Oh my God, you bought that for me! For my thirtieth. I remember! And Becca and the girls came up. Holy shit, I remember . . . Sophie's all big now!"

I laughed. "My God, Juss. Those memories are all over the years."

He was teary again. "They're not in any order. Nothing kinda makes sense, and it's random as hell. Makes my head hurt, not gonna lie."

I put my hand to his forehead. "Do you feel okay?"

He gave me a smile. "No, nothing like that. I feel great. My head's still foggy, but something obviously cleared up. Just feels . . . like the hinges on the memory door could use some WD-40, that's all."

I barked out a laugh. "What about some coffee?"

He smiled. "Suppose. Even decaf."

As much as I wanted to stay in bed with him, I knew we couldn't. "You have an engine to finish today, remember?"

He brightened. "Oh shit, yes." He rolled away from me and sat on the edge of the bed. "You make the coffees. I need to pee."

I watched him get up and limp-walk out to the bathroom across the hall. He would never stop amazing me.

He paused at the door and turned to face me. "I can't believe you bought me the KTM. You never told me that when we talked about it."

"Because I'm not supposed to plant memories. You were so stoked that you finally owned a KTM, I didn't want to tell you in the hospital I bought it for you in case you thought you owed me something. I had to be careful with how I worded things, that's all."

He frowned now. "Yeah, sorry. I'm not blaming you for not telling me. I just can't believe you bought it for me."

I chuckled. "It wasn't brand new when I got it. I couldn't afford brand new."

"I don't care about that," he added quickly. "It's new to me. And now it's new to me again." He snorted. "Anyway, it just means the sooner I can ride it, the better."

I laughed to hide the horror I felt at that thought. "I bought it because it was your dream to own one. But how about we wait for the riding part. I don't think we're there yet." I put my hand to my chest. "Not sure my heart could take it."

He grinned like that was a challenge, then turned back toward the bathroom. "I need to pee."

I chuckled as I got out of bed and pulled on some shorts. I didn't dare hope that we were getting back to how we used to be, but this was us, this was us before the accident—aside from him telling me every time he needed to pee. That was new. And funny. And kind of a very Justin thing to do.

The memory development was amazing. But his emotional connection, his emotional memory, what he felt about me, how he could feel how very real we were . . . well, that was better than any memory to me.

That was everything.

———

CHAPTER SIX

THE NEXT WEEK was filled with small improvements. Justin could get rid of the collar-cuff-sling thing he hated so much, and he was walking more and more. He still used the scooter, mostly around the workshop, but in the unit he was on his feet. He tried to use a crutch, but it aggravated his arm and he got frustrated with it in about ten seconds and went back to the scooter.

I'd joked with his physiotherapist it was all about the wheels. *If you want to make Justin happy, give the man some wheels.*

He'd been back to the neurologist, and the doc was happy with Justin's health. He'd had a session with Doctor Chang, and she was so happy with his improvements and regained memories she almost cried. Or maybe that was because Justin got all teary when he was telling her and she welled up in sympathy. He'd remembered a few other things during the week. All small, seemingly inconsequential and random things, like a pair of shoes, when we'd gone to the races and he'd won fifty bucks on a horse, and when

Squish was a kitten. But every tiny piece of the puzzle made the picture a little clearer.

He'd finished working on the two old engines we'd dubbed his therapy puzzles and had begun helping Sparra with some small jobs. He never pushed himself, though, and he knew his limits because he knew all too well if he went too hard for too long, he'd be absolute cactus the whole next day.

So he put in a few hours every morning and called it quits every day when his nurse arrived. He'd have lunch and a nap on the couch with Squish, and he'd begun cooking dinner before I came upstairs.

He'd even searched a few recipes on his phone, and that was a real sign to me that he was improving. He was using initiative and thinking ahead. After the accident, Justin had been in such a foggy daze, he would just sit and wait, agreeing to whatever I suggested. Now he was reading more and watching more shows on TV that required brainpower.

It was easy to believe things were . . . improving. I didn't want to say 'returning to normal' or 'going back to what they were' because that was never going to happen. The accident had changed him forever. It had changed us forever. But right now, we were in a real good place; Justin was getting better and stronger every day, he was happier, and we'd hold hands and snuggle on the couch, he'd cling to me in his sleep, and we'd kissed a handful of times.

It was just like dating all over again.

And in many ways, it was sweeter the second time around. It wasn't all about sex now, which it had been the first time. We'd fallen hard and fast and couldn't keep our hands off each other back then. Now we were taking things slow and learning about each other.

Sure, I woke up with a hard-on most days, but that was

just my body reacting to him being wrapped around me. I was very content with keeping things slow between us. Justin seemed oblivious to my morning wood, and he never seemed curious about sex at all. He wasn't ready, physically, mentally, or emotionally anyway, and being cosied up with him on the couch and kissing and giggling in the ad breaks was all kinds of perfect for me.

If that was all we ever did for the rest of our lives, I'd be a happy, happy man.

On the Friday night, Justin had cooked dinner, and I'd cleaned up while he chatted with his sister, Becca, and the girls on the phone. The weather had turned cool, so he was settled on the couch with a blanket, and I joined him soon after with a bowl of popcorn just as the football was starting.

Justin was staring at the screen but not really looking at it.

"How was Bec?" I asked.

"Oh." He turned to me and smiled. "Yeah, she's good. Busy."

"And the girls?"

"They're great. Loud, to be honest. I dunno how Bec does it."

I chuckled but he seemed distracted. "Everything okay?"

"Yeah . . . just tired."

It was the end of the week, that was true, and he'd been walking more. But I wasn't convinced. "Yeah. Looking forward to the weekend. Did you want to do anything in particular?"

He studied the TV for a long second. "Not really. I dunno."

"Juss, you feel okay?"

"Yeah, of course," he said, affording me a smile that didn't seem to sit right. "Sorry. Tired and over . . . thinking."

Okay so there hadn't been much word confusion lately, until now, and he was out of sorts. I slid the popcorn onto the coffee table and pulled a cushion onto my lap and patted it. "Lie down, baby."

He lay down with his head on my lap, without a word, without any facial expression. Just robotically, the way he was a few weeks ago. I gently ran my fingers through his hair, and not even twenty seconds later, he was asleep. I managed to pull my phone from my pocket without waking him and sent Bec a quick text.

Hey, when you spoke to Juss earlier, was he okay?

Her reply came through half a minute later. *Was okay. Said he'd had a great week but was tired. But then I might have put my foot in something . . . sorry.*

Well, that was never good.

About what?

I asked him if the sex was better the second time around. I meant it as a joke. We'd always talked about that stuff before, Dallas. I'm sorry. He went real quiet. Said he had to go. I'm so sorry.

Fuck, fuck, shit fuck.

It's okay, Bec. He's asleep right now. Will talk to him about it. Give the girls a kiss for me.

Thanks, Dall. Again, I'm really sorry xx

So yes, he was tired. He'd had a really busy week. He'd been productive and he'd made huge strides in his recovery and he was exhausted.

But one mention of sex had knocked him down a peg. Maybe it was my fault for not talking to him about that and asking him if he had any questions. Maybe he'd been trying to figure stuff out in his head and couldn't get the puzzle pieces to fit.

I traced my fingers through his hair and studied his profile. He looked so peaceful. His full lips were parted, his long eyelashes cast perfect shadows, his stubbled jaw, his perfect nose.

There was also the new scar above his eyebrow and the long L-shaped surgical scar along the side of his head. It was hidden by his hair now, though I could see it this close up. I could even see the staple punctures that ran along the outside, making it look like a skin-coloured centipede from a Tim Burton movie.

And yet, he was still beautiful.

I loved him more now than I ever had.

"Hey, baby," I whispered, rousing him gently. "Time for bed."

He cracked one eye and grumbled, but he sat up. It was slow and measured, and I doubted he'd be getting to bed unassisted, so I got to my feet and helped him to his. He all but fell into me, so I helped him to the hall. "Bathroom first?"

It took a second for him to answer. "Yep."

"You okay by yourself, or do you need me to help?"

His brow furrowed but he didn't answer. He just shuffled into the bathroom. So I turned down the bed and waited for him to pee and brush his teeth. I helped him undress and he got into bed wearing just his briefs and I pulled the covers up.

"You stay," he mumbled, his eyes closed.

"Of course," I whispered. "I'll just turn everything off and be straight in."

He was already out of it, so I turned the bedroom light off and went back out to the living room. It was still early and I wasn't exactly tired, so I tidied up a bit and watched some of the footy. I straightened up the couch, fixing cushions and folding the blanket. Justin's journal was on the coffee table and I left it untouched, but the photos I'd given him weeks ago when he was in hospital were in a pile there as well.

He'd always kept them close by, looking through them periodically. He'd remembered a few of the images and what he'd been doing at the time. But I couldn't help but notice the photos of him and me together were at the top of the pile. The one where we were all dressed up and posing for the camera; the one where we were on the couch, laughing. And the one of us in our bed, his naked torso sweaty and flushed. It was pretty clear what was going on in that photo and he'd picked it straight away. Not that he remembered that particular memory—or any memory of us being intimate, for that matter—but he knew what intimacy looked like. He knew it was us in that photo and that he was bottoming. He even said he was glad that hadn't changed. That he was still the same. He knew all this, but I guess he never put it all together until now. I'd noticed these photos had been looked through more this week. I just assumed he was becoming more familiar with the images and the few memories he'd recovered.

The poor guy had probably been trying to figure out everything on his own. And knowing Justin, he'd probably been stressing over it but didn't want to ask.

We'd definitely have to have a chat tomorrow.

No longer interested in the football game, I turned the TV off, and by the time I'd done my teeth and changed into some sleep shorts, I was grateful for the early night. I slipped in beside Justin, and as soon as my head hit my pillow, he stirred and shuffled over and snuggled into me.

I wrapped an arm around him and kissed his forehead. "Love you, Juss."

I wasn't expecting a response. I thought he was asleep. But his reply came fast and quiet. "Love you, Dall."

My heart came to a screeching halt and I froze, yet his breaths were deep and measured. He was sound asleep. His words had come so fast and so sure, it was like the old Justin. It was something the old Justin and I had said to each other a thousand times. In fact, it was our usual goodnight to each other.

Had something in his sleeping mind answered for him? Without his conscious brain being aware, had some part of his hippocampus relaxed and let a memory slip through? I had no idea. I'd have to ask Doctor Chang during the week.

But right now, I turned into Justin and held him so much tighter.

Love you, Dall.

I fell asleep smiling and I reckon I woke up much the same way.

CHAPTER SEVEN

I HAD coffee and toast on the table when Juss came out of the bedroom. He was walking, no scooter, with his hair all messed up and a scowl on his face. His angry-puppy face was so adorable in the morning, and it made me smile.

"Morning," I said, trying not to be too cheerful.

"Hmm," he said as he huffed onto a seat at the table, mindful of his leg. "Morning."

I slid his coffee closer, then his plate of toast. "Sleep okay?"

"Hmm." He sipped his brew and tried a bite of toast. "Yeah."

I smiled behind my coffee cup. I'd always loved his pouty morning face. It was like a puppy learning how to growl. But today I loved it even more. I was still on a high from last night.

He told me he loved me.

So what if he was asleep? His sleeping brain had let a truth trickle out, and I was gonna hold onto that forever.

"What did you want to do this arvo?" I asked. "Supposed to be a nice day out."

He shrugged a shoulder as he sipped his coffee. "Dunno."

"I have some stuff to do downstairs this morning, but I thought maybe we could go and have some fish and chips on the beach for lunch. Sound okay?"

Another bite of toast, another sip of coffee, then the hint of a smile. "Sounds good."

It never took him too long to come to grips with being awake. "I'm gonna go have a quick shower."

"'Kay."

Thirty minutes later, we were both showered, the kitchen was tidied, and I was helping Juss down the stairs. He was getting better and stronger every day. Small steps every day didn't seem like much, but in hindsight, looking back to a week or a fortnight, he really had come far.

He used the scooter in the workshop because the shed itself was huge, with flat concrete floors he could zip around on. He was using his arm more now he'd gotten rid of the collar-cuff. He still couldn't lift anything heavy with it or even hold it out for too long, but he could use it. He had physio exercises for it, and every so often I'd see him rotate his wrist or open and close his fingers.

Always trying to improve.

Such an old-Justin thing to do. Though I really had to stop thinking of him as two different people. There shouldn't be an old and a new Justin. There was just this Justin. My Justin. This was who he was now.

And as soon as I had the roller door up, he made himself busy, cleaning, tidying, sweeping while I ducked into my office. I'd fully caught up on my paperwork, debtors and creditors, orders, and whatnot. We'd completed the Simpson contract and had been paid, which was a relief and took some pressure off. But what I hadn't done was finalise the insurance claim on the van. Or, rather, the insurance company hadn't.

I checked my emails and sighed when there was no reply to my request for an update. I even checked the spam and junk folders. There was nothing. I'd been told that workers' comp and insurance claims could take an eternity, but my case manager was hopeful for a quick turnaround.

Apparently not.

And it wasn't just the van, but the several thousand dollars' worth of tools, equipment, and fit-out in the back of the van that we'd lost as well. None of that was salvageable, and it had been a huge financial loss. After a few weeks of scraping by, things at the shop weren't getting back on track as fast as I'd hoped. And the very last thing I wanted to do was have Justin be worrying over bloody money and having guilt impede his recovery.

Justin's face appeared at the door. "Uh, Dallas? There's a guy pulled up out the front. He's coming in."

The shop was technically closed, and the only people who called past to see us on a weekend were our friends. I followed him out and, sure enough, saw Simmo at the front gate. It was locked, so I went to let him in.

"Long time no see," I said, unlocking the padlock.

"Was just driving through. Thought I'd call in and see how you guys were getting on."

Simmo had worked as a parts rep for years and he used to call in at least once a week. He was a real good bloke and a knockabout kinda guy who loved bikes and motocross as much as us, and over the years, he'd become a mate. He got promoted two years ago to some regional area management role and spent most of his time crunching numbers now instead of riding, but he'd call in every chance he got just for a chat and a laugh.

"We're good," I said, locking the gate behind him. "All things considered. We're doing real good."

He looked over at the workshop and kept his voice low. "How's Justin?"

"He's doing okay. Simmo, I dunno if he'll remember you. He didn't remember Davo or Sparra, so . . ." I gave him a smile. "Let's go find out. He was pushing a broom around last I saw him."

We walked back into the workshop, and sure enough, Justin was on his scooter pushing the broom in front of him. He looked a little too into it, and I kinda got the feeling he might have been watching us chat at the gate and now he was trying to act like he hadn't been. That made me smile.

"Hey, Jusso," I said and waited for him to scoot over. "Do you remember Simmo?"

Justin's gaze went from me to Simmo, then back to me. He shook his head. "No, sorry . . ."

"That's okay," I said brightly. "Justin, this is Luke Simpson. We call him Simmo."

Justin gingerly held out his right hand, and Simmo could obviously see that and thankfully, he shook it gently. "G'day," Juss replied. "Did I . . . ? Did I know you before?"

Simmo glanced at me, then gave a nod. "Yeah, mate."

"Sorry." Justin frowned and gestured loosely to his own head. "I'm missing a few years. Brain got a faulty recalibration."

I chuckled and Simmo laughed. "But you haven't changed much," Simmo said. Then he motioned toward his scooter. "New wheels."

"Yeah, not as fast and four wheels instead of two, but it'll have to do," he replied.

It was then Simmo noticed the scars down Juss' leg. "Holy shit, Jusso."

"Yep," he said, smiling at how Simmo called him that. "Matches the one in my head." He pointed to the scar above his ear.

"Fuck," Simmo breathed, going in for a closer look. "Ouch."

They began talking about scars and surgeries and laughing about stupid shit. It was funny how they were kind of only meeting again now for the first time but still talking like old friends.

Human brains were strange and complex things.

And Simmo was probably the first person to call around to see him as a friend, apart from Davo and Sparra, of course. It was good to see how Justin reacted to meeting someone he guessed he knew before the accident but had no memory of. It didn't seem to upset him at all. He just rolled with it.

I guess this was his new normal.

There was just so much he had to roll with because he didn't have a choice.

And as he took Simmo over to his KTM and showed it to him like he hadn't already seen it, I fell in love with him a little bit more. And Simmo, God bless him, just went with it too. Justin had just given Simmo the rundown on the engine capacity and torque specs, which of course he already knew.

"You've probably seen all this before," Jussy said, a little embarrassed now. "Sorry."

"Nah, mate. Don't apologise," Simmo said. "I'd be excited too if it were mine. And anyway, I could talk about bikes all day long."

Justin smiled. "Same."

"So have they told you when you can ride again?" he asked.

Juss looked to me. "No. Did they tell you, Dallas?"

"No, they haven't said, but if his doctors have any say, it'll be never," I answered with a smile. "But we'll get there."

Justin grinned at me. "Yeah. We will."

"Did you get the insurance sorted from the accident?" Simmo asked.

Shit.

My gaze shot to Justin, something neither of them missed. "Uh, not yet. Still waiting. All the reports were done and in our favour. But you know how insurance and workers' comp are."

Simmo gave me a strained, sorry look. "Yeah, terrible on a good day. Keep on them, though. Squeaky wheel and all that, ya know?"

"Yeah, it's just all red tape and paperwork," I said. "Shouldn't be too much longer."

"Good," he said, then gave Juss a clap on the shoulder. "It's real good to see you up and about. And next time I come through, I wanna see you on that KTM."

Justin smiled and they said their goodbyes, though I knew Justin would have questions for me. I walked Simmo to the gate. "Shit, man," he began. "I'm sorry for bringing the insurance up. I didn't think . . ."

"Nah, it's okay. I just don't want him to stress over it. He has enough to worry about."

"He's doing okay, though, yeah? I mean, he's had more stitches than a baseball."

That made me smile. "He's doing much better, now. Early days were touch and go, but he's made some great progress. He's remembering bits and pieces, which is great."

He shook his head. "Crazy how it can all change so quick, huh?"

"Oh yeah. Every single thing." I snapped my fingers. "Just like that."

He sighed and offered me his hand before he slipped out the gate with promises to see us again soon. I waved him off and walked back up to the workshop, knowing I'd have to face Justin's questions at some point.

But he wasn't sitting on his scooter anymore. He was sitting on his motorbike. I baulked. "Uh, what do you think you're doing?"

"Just wanted to see how it feels," he replied.

I didn't want to know how he got his leg over it. Christ. The idea of him riding a bike again so soon damn near gave me heart failure. I relaxed when I remembered he couldn't start it, at least. He didn't have the key. "How does it feel?"

"Feels good." He held the handlebars and cranked the throttle. "Feels familiar . . . but it's not. I don't remember it, like this bike exactly, but it feels right."

"Well, you look great. How does your leg feel?"

He glanced down at his injured leg, then up at me. "This feels okay. No way I could ride yet, though."

"Not gonna lie, kinda glad to hear that," I admitted. "Not sure my heart could take it just yet." I'd said it with a smile, as a bit of a joke, but it was the truth. If he took any kind of fall off a bike, if he hit his head, even with a helmet . . . I shuddered at the thought.

"But you said I look good," he replied with a cheeky smirk.

"Shut up. You always looked good on a bike and you know it."

He laughed. "I do not. And anyway, I couldn't ride it yet because I don't think I can even get off it without some help."

I snorted and helped him, holding onto him while he

manoeuvred his leg. When he was back on his own two feet, he was standing impossibly close and my arm was still around him. He looked up at me. "You could kiss me right now," he whispered.

I didn't need telling twice.

I cupped his jaw and brought his mouth to mine, kissing him, opening his mouth with mine and tasting his tongue. I felt his surprise give way as he melted into me and he kissed me back. I could have stayed right there forever. I could have kissed him like that until we both ran out of air. How easy it would have been to take it one step further, to pull him in close and grind against him, to slip a hand between us and grip him . . .

I pulled away, breaking the kiss far too abruptly and far too soon for my liking. He was dazed, his jaw slack, his eyes heavy-lidded, his lips wet.

"You okay?" I breathed.

"Uhm." He blinked and a slow smile toyed with his lips. "Wow."

I chuckled. "I could say the same." I pecked his lips once more, soft and sweet. "Did you still want to go to the beach for lunch? We can do it another day if you want."

"No, today'd be great."

"Sure? We've had a busy week."

"Yeah, I'm sure." He sighed. "It's weird. And difficult, I guess."

I took his hand. "What is?"

"The need to rest, and not wanting to waste any more time." He shrugged his good shoulder. "I have a lot to catch up on, and don't want to waste a day, but I know I need to take it easy or it puts me on my arse for two days."

"There's a balance, and I think we're doing okay. I'll do

whatever you want to do, baby, but the second you've had enough, you need to tell me."

He rolled his eyes. "I don't need to tell you nothing. You know when I'm tired before I do."

I laughed, guilty as charged. "Maybe." I could tell him every sign; the way his right eye blinked slower than his left, or the way his words were slower and a little slurred when he was really tired, the way it took a second for him to answer. All these things had improved so much, lessened with every day, but they were still there when he'd reached his limit. "Come on, then, let's go now. Sooner we go, the sooner we can come back. I wouldn't even mind a nap on the couch this arvo. Then the footy starts at four, then dinner, maybe a movie. I'll even let you pick it if you like."

He smiled and shook his head.

"What?"

"Nothing," he answered.

"Does that sound lame to you? Did you want to do something else? We can do something else if you want."

"God, Dallas, no. That sounds amazing. Lunch at the beach, a nap, footy, dinner, a movie. It's . . . Well, it sounds perfect." His face softened and there was something in his eyes . . . something that looked a lot like happiness. "Yes, I know this is nothing new to you, but it is to me. We like the same things, and you want to spend your day off doing the same things I like to do. I don't wanna do anything fancy; I just wanna hang out, and I'm still getting used to the fact that you want to do that with me. I just . . . it just blows me away, that's all. Like I can't believe it. Like I've woken up in some dream."

I sighed as I smiled and put my hands to his face. "It's no dream, Juss. We got lucky when we found each other. Well, I got lucky the day you walked in here. We never had to pretend to be something we're not. We just . . . we were just right, from day one."

He closed his eyes, and when I thought he might kiss me, he ducked his head and put his arms around me instead. I wrapped him up in a hug and rubbed his back, and he took deep, measured breaths. "Thank you," he murmured. "For everything. I don't know where I'd be if it weren't for you."

"You'd be just fine, Juss. You're stronger than you know." I planted a kiss on the side of his head and pulled back. "I'll just run upstairs and grab everything. Won't be long."

Ten minutes later, we were on our way to Merewether Beach. It was going to be busy. Sure, it was winter, but the sun was out and people would be enjoying the Saturday sunshine. But the access paths were concrete and relatively flat for Justin's scooter and there were a lot of grassed areas at Dixon Park we could sit on. I highly doubted he'd be up for walking on sandy beaches just yet.

I still drove carefully, more aware of having Justin in the ute with me and of how he might react to certain situations in traffic. I dreaded what memories the sound of screeching tyres or honking horns might bring out, but thankfully it was uneventful.

We ordered fish and chips from the kiosk, then found a parking spot at Dixon Park and I went around to Justin's side of the ute and took his scooter from out of the back. I helped him out, and while he got himself sorted on that, I collected the picnic blanket and pillows. When I locked the ute and joined him on the footpath, he had his eyes closed and was smiling up toward the sun.

Christ, he was beautiful.

"Feel good?" I asked.

"Feels amazing. The sun, the smell of the saltwater. Everything."

After spending weeks in a hospital bed and then the last few weeks seeing nothing but our flat, the work shed, or doctors' offices, I bet it all felt amazing. "Then let's find a spot and you can lie down and enjoy it."

So that's what we did.

We found a secluded spot not far from the ute, over-looking the Pacific Ocean. I laid the blanket out, threw the pillows down, and helped him sit down. We sat and ate our lunch, watching the beach for a bit, watched the pulse of the ocean ebb and flow. We watched people walking dogs, pushing prams, throwing frisbees, jogging . . . The winter sun was just warm enough, the breeze was cool, and it was a perfect reminder to enjoy the little things.

Just to take a minute to breathe.

We lay in the sun with our heads on the pillows and pointed out shapes in the clouds. Then he asked me ques-tions about things he'd missed in the last five years. Things from who the Prime Minister was and which famous people had died, and a bunch of little things that made me realise his mind was getting clearer.

These were questions he wouldn't have thought to ask two weeks ago, but now he was wondering about things outside our lives. And that was a very good sign. I thought he might ask me about sex, and I knew it was something we'd have to discuss, but instead, he asked me something else.

"And what's happening with the insurance with the accident?" he asked. "That guy Simmo asked, and I should have known to ask before now."

I rolled onto my side to face him and tucked the pillow under my neck. "I don't expect you to ask," I replied gently.

"Though maybe I should have told you before now so you didn't have to ask. The insurance is taking longer than I thought. They keep saying it's just procedure and how these things take time, but I can't get anyone to return my calls, and when they do, they tell me there's no progress to report."

"Is that normal?"

"Apparently. But still, it's a pain."

He frowned and chewed on his bottom lip. "Are we . . . do we need the money?"

Shit. I couldn't lie to him.

"Things are tight. We're okay for now, but if we don't get it soon, we might have to look at some options."

"Such as?"

"Asking the bank to lessen the loan repayments, getting a redraw, extending credit cards, that kind of thing. But we're not there just yet." I reached over and took his hand. "I didn't tell you because I didn't want you to worry. Doctor Chang said that stress and anxiety can impede your recovery and that's the last thing I want to do."

"But the accident . . ."

"The accident was exactly that. An accident. It wasn't anyone's fault. Certainly not yours, and the insurance company and workers' comp all know that; they've all agreed to that. It's just a matter of the paperwork being signed off on, I'm sure." I skimmed my thumb over his knuckles. "The van, the fit-out, the tools, and your wages and the medical bills will all be covered. It's just a matter of time, that's all."

"I don't want you to have money troubles, Dallas." He was still frowning. "After everything you've done for me."

"Hey, Jussy. It's just paperwork. We'll get it sorted. It's just a matter of juggling things until then."

"I hate that it's a problem though." He chewed on his bottom lip for a long moment. "I could sell my bike."

"You what?"

"My bike."

"No."

"I can't ride it right now," he said, frowning. "I know you bought it for me and I love that you did. But it's the least I could do. It's all I own. If we need the money . . ."

Oh my God, that broke my heart. "No, Juss. No. We don't need to do that."

This was why I hadn't wanted him to know about it. Because he would worry, even if I told him there was nothing to worry about. There was no way I could tell him about having stock orders cancelled because of unpaid accounts.

I needed to change the subject, get his mind off worrying.

"You know what I realised?" I asked. "When you were lying in that hospital bed and you still hadn't opened your eyes, and we didn't know if you ever would at that stage, the boys were manning the workshop taking care of everything for us. It was very clear to me what my priorities were. If it came down to it, if I had to choose, I'd choose you. No matter the cost. No matter the sacrifice. I'd choose you, Juss. And right now, if I had to choose again, it'd still be you. And every day in between, and every day from now till forever."

His eyes became glassy and he gave me a sad smile. "Can I tell you something?"

"Sure."

"When I was in hospital and they talked about sending me home, I was shit scared. I didn't know you, but I knew I could trust you. I could feel it. I just knew. There was something in your eyes that was so honest." He swallowed hard and let out a shaky breath. "So I had to choose: go home with you or find my own place. I chose you, and if I had to choose again today, I'd choose you. You are my home, Dall."

"Oh, baby." I kissed his knuckles. "Thank you."

"Five years ago, or whenever we met, I chose you the first time." His dark brown eyes shone in the sun. "And I choose you again. This second time . . . well, second time for you, first time for me, really." He laughed nervously; a blush crept over his cheeks. "So does this make us boyfriends? Even though we live together and have been together for five years. And I can't seem to sleep without you. But maybe we should make it official?"

I grinned while my heart banged around in my chest. "Uh, yeah. Yes, definitely. I mean, I'd really like that."

He laughed. "Me too. I'd choose you again a third time too, just so you know."

I leaned over and kissed him, which wasn't easy considering I was grinning like an idiot. "You just made me so freaking happy."

He covered his eyes with his hand and laughed again. When he peeked through his fingers, his eyes were like glittered bronze. "You really want to be my boyfriend?"

I scrambled to my knees and sat back on my haunches and let out a happy sigh. "More than anything in the world."

Justin sat up slowly, careful of both his leg and his arm. "You just made me really freaking happy too." He looked out at the ocean, smiling. "Boyfriends, huh. Kinda feels weird. I always wanted a boyfriend. Someone just to hang out with. Someone who gets me. And now I have that. Except I've had it all along. Sort of." Then he let out a bit of a chuckle. "I mean, it's new and exciting but familiar and comfortable, so I guess I get the best of both worlds."

I cupped his face and pressed my lips to his. "I remember every single thing, Juss. And it's new and exciting but familiar and comfortable for me too."

He slow blinked, still smiling, but he'd had enough. "How about we get going home?" I suggested. "I have a nap in my future."

Justin snorted. "Me too."

I jumped to my feet and took his left hand, pulling him to his feet. I waited a moment for his head to catch up. "You okay? Not too dizzy?"

He slow blinked again. "Nah. 'M okay."

We got everything packed up and back to the ute just fine, but he was asleep in the car before we got halfway home.

CHAPTER EIGHT

THE MORNING VENTURE had taken its toll and as soon as I got him upstairs, he made it to the couch and put his feet up on the recliner and fell straight back to sleep. I pulled the blanket over him and turned the TV on, volume low for background noise while I got some housework done.

Later on, I'd thrown a bunch of meat and veg into the slow cooker hoping for some kind of Irish stew, and when I walked past the couch, Juss was awake.

He was squinting and frowning.

"Hey," I whispered. "You feel okay?"

He paused for a long moment, then gave a slight shake of his head. "Headache."

I fetched him some pills and a glass of water, then closed the blinds. I found the remote for the TV and went into settings and turned the brightness way down. "Is that better?"

He sagged back against the sofa and closed his eyes. "Hm."

Squish recognised Justin's bat-signal and trotted over to curl up with him. I gave Squish a scratch for thanks and pressed a kiss to Juss' forehead. "If you need anything, just ask," I whispered.

I cleaned the bathroom, changed the bedsheets, and remade the bed, trying to be as quiet as I could. About an hour later, he had his eyes open but was staring absently at the TV. I sat beside him and watched the screen for a bit. Turning the brightness down actually made a lot of difference and it was less straining to look at. It was on some billiards highlights that he wasn't really watching. "How're you feeling?"

"'M okay," he said slowly.

His hand was between us, so I traced patterns on his palm with my finger. "Can I get you anything?"

He blinked. "Nah." Then after a long while, he added, "Just sit with me."

His speech was a little slower than it had been the last few days, and I was reminded that his recovery was two steps forward, one step back. Just like Doctor Chang had said it would be.

"I'll sit with you anytime," I whispered, and his fingers curled into mine.

"Headache was bad," he mumbled.

"But it's okay now?"

He gave a small nod. "Better."

Better, but still there, obviously. And even if the pain had been dulled, the residual effects weren't lessened. The spaced-out fogginess remained.

Squish stretched out and Juss rubbed his belly with his other hand, and he looked up at me and smiled. "I like this."

"Like what? Being all cosy on the couch with the cat?"

He slow blinked again, and he smiled at me. "Yeah. With my boyfriend. I haven't forgotten that."

I grinned, then leant over and kissed him. "I haven't

forgotten either." I snuggled in a bit closer and his head fell against my shoulder, our fingers still entwined. It had grown overcast outside, so it really was a perfect way to spend a cold and blustery afternoon; cosied up on the couch, Squish purring between us, the footy about to start, and dinner cooking away in the kitchen.

"Did you say the Bulldogs were playing?"

"Yep. Be prepared to watch the best team in the NRL."

He chuckled. "The Knights aren't playing."

The game began and I got us some snacks and a bottle of water each, and he enjoyed the game but he seemed a little distracted. The Bulldogs ended up winning, though even I wasn't sure how, and I served up our stew, which we ate on the couch.

He was speaking better and his blinks were fine, so I believed him when he said his head was feeling okay, though he seemed to have something on his mind. He'd look at me, then at the TV, and he chewed more on his bottom lip than he did of his dinner.

"Is there something you wanted to talk about?" I asked, trying to be casual.

He smiled. "That's not fair."

"What's not fair?"

"That you know me. You can tell these things because you know me."

I laughed. "Sorry."

He ate some more dinner and I gave him time to get his thoughts in order. "I've been thinking," he began. "Well, trying to anyway. And I know I probably should have asked before now."

"You can ask me anything," I tried.

"Then Becca said something the other night . . ."

Oh shit. Here we go. The sex talk.

But I couldn't let him be the one to struggle to bring this up. That most certainly wasn't fair. "She told me. She was worried that she'd said something to upset you. Juss, I want you to know, there is no pressure for anything physical between us."

He made a face and studied his bowl of stew for a bit. "I know we kinda talked about it before. You said I still bottomed so that was one thing that hadn't changed."

I snorted and put my bowl onto the coffee table. "Ah, yeah."

"And the photo . . . of us. Of me. It's pretty obvious what you're doing to me . . ."

"I wasn't going to put that photo in but Bec thought it might show you that you and I were a couple," I said. "Sorry if it upset you."

"No, not upset. I like the photo," he replied, blushing and smiling all shy-like. "But . . ."

Oh. "But what?"

His lip drew downward. "I haven't thought about it. Sex, that is. I haven't thought about it, not once. I haven't wanted it," he said eventually. "And I don't know why."

"Because your body isn't ready yet," I offered. "Your brain needs time."

"Maybe," he mumbled. "Do you think . . . do you think something broke? In my brain?"

I scooted over and took his hand. "Baby, no. You'll want it when you're ready. And I don't care when that is. Tomorrow, or ten years, or never. Sex isn't the reason I love you."

He sighed and leaned against the back of the sofa, holding my hand and looking at me all gooey. It did crazy things to my heart. "You make it easy, you know," he whispered.

"Make what easy?"

"To fall in love with you."

I stared.

My heart stopped.

My mouth fell open. "What?"

He laughed and ducked his head. "Don't make me say it again."

I was so fucking giddy I almost vibrated off the couch. I grabbed his face and planted a kiss on his mouth. "I love you, Juss. Always have, always will."

His eyes unfocused, just for a second. "Whoa," he whispered. "I think I just had a flashback." He blinked a few times. "You've said that before."

I grinned. "I've said it a hundred times."

"No, you were wearing a black hoodie and we were outside. At the beach." His eyes grew wide. "I remember that. Oh my God, Dallas, I remember that."

Black hoodie . . . at the beach . . . "Yes, at Hallidays Point. Our weekend away."

Then his eyes glimmered with something else and his cheeks grew red. "Oh. I think I remember something else . . ." He put his hand to his forehead. "Oh yeah. There was a couch and a blue bed . . ."

Oh God . . . I'd bent him over that couch and fucked him until he came. He'd begged me to do it. He'd leaned himself over the back of the couch and undid his pants, offering me his arse. He'd writhed with need, and he'd begged me. Was he remembering that?

The blush on his cheeks told me yes.

And that big blue bed . . . we barely left it all weekend.

"Yeah," I said, my voice rough. "There was. You remember it?"

He nodded and let out a ragged breath. "Fuck. Parts of it, I think. God, we uh . . . I mean, you . . ."

I chuckled and tried to take a calming breath. "Uh, yeah."

He sat back, and from the slightly bewildered and embarrassed look on his face, I could tell he was reliving his new memories. And they were memories that included me, which made me ridiculously happy.

"You got new memories," I said, lifting his hand to kiss his palm.

But then he put his fingers to my chin, he thumbed my beard, savouring the texture and tugging on it a little, his eyes taking in all the details. "I remember. I remember what we did and how you made me feel." He swallowed hard. "It's not just the visual, it's the emotion that goes with it. That makes it real, and I can feel what I felt back then, how you made me feel. That's *my* memories, not photos, not what someone says happened. Me, mine." He was breathing hard; his chest rose and fell with each beat of my own. "You."

"Me? Me what?"

"You made me feel that way. You. Christ, Dallas. I remember what we did."

I took his hand and held it in both of mine. "I remember too. The beauty of it, the love."

He nodded, but then he licked his lips and shook his head. "I don't know what it means." He swallowed hard again. "No, I know what it means. I mean, I know what we did and I know how it made me feel. I remember wanting it so bad I thought I was going to combust."

I laughed. "Same."

"But I don't know what that means for me now."

"What do you mean, baby?"

"I haven't thought about sex in . . . well, since the accident. I mean, yeah, I know we used to have sex, and I get that. But I haven't thought about actually doing it. I haven't wanted to. Not once."

I lifted his hand and kissed his knuckles this time. "That's okay, baby."

"Is it?"

"Sure it is. It'll happen when you're ready. Maybe it's your brain's way of making sure you're ready first." I took a deep breath. "Baby, you had a shit time in Darwin. And before that, here in Newcastle. Guys treated you like shit, expecting a quick fuck and nothing else, and all you wanted was someone to love you. When we first got together, you were adamant that you wanted trust and respect, and rightly so. It's not any different this time around. When your body and your heart, and your mind, are all ready, you'll know."

His gaze flickered between mine and he opened his mouth to say something, but then he closed it again. He shook his head. "How can you just say that?"

"Say what?"

"Be so understanding!"

"Because I love you. I'm not going to rush you and risk ruining what we have just to get off. I told you before, you mean more to me than just sex."

Juss' eyebrows furrowed and he sank back in his seat. "I don't get it. I keep expecting you to get pissed off or frustrated, but you never do. It's like you're too perfect or something."

I snorted out a laugh. "Hardly. I'm far from it. But Juss, I know what we had, and I know it's worth it. You're worth it, what we had, and what we have right now, is worth it."

He gave me a sad smile. "There you go being all perfect again."

"I'm not perfect. I'm just looking after you, like I know

you would if it had been me in that van that day. You would've moved heaven and earth for me. I know you would have."

He got a little teary. After a little while, he said, "I guess I just don't know . . ."

"Don't know what, baby?"

"How you love me when I don't know who I am. I feel half put together with missing pieces, yet you still love me, and I don't know how I can love you when I don't know who I'm supposed to be or who you fell in love with. And what if that guy isn't who I am?"

"Oh, Juss. I love the real you." I put my hand to his chest. "The guy who laughs at blooper videos, and the guy who was scared to death to put his heart on the line but did it anyway. The guy who rescued a little black kitten and fed him every three or four hours for weeks. The guy who stood up to shitty men because he demanded better; the guy who worked his arse off to be better than anyone else to prove that a gay man could do it. That's who you are."

A solitary tear escaped his eye. "You can stop being perfect now."

"I'm not perfect," I said again, wiping his cheek. "I'm far from it. I just love you, that's all."

He gave a teary laugh and leaned in to kiss me. But then, without breaking the kiss, he slid closer on the couch and deepened the kiss. I couldn't hide my surprise when he climbed into my lap and kissed me so thoroughly it made my eyes roll back in my head. I didn't want him to force himself to *try*, but damnit it felt so good...

And then he rubbed himself against me and I had to put my hands on his hips to stop him. I held him off me and broke the kiss, his forehead pressed to mine. "Stop," I breathed. "I'm not *that* perfect."

He almost smirked. "Oh, sorry."

I shifted in my seat and gently pushed him off my lap. Then I had to readjust myself, my now-aching dick protesting his absence. I grimaced. "Don't be sorry. It's just . . . my dick doesn't understand."

He stared at me, then burst out laughing. He covered his mouth with his hand. "I'm sorry. That's not funny."

"Then why are you laughing?" I asked. I couldn't help but smile. It was so good to see him laugh.

He let his hand drop and he stared at me; his whole face lit up with a grin. "I dunno, I just . . . you're turned on, by me. It's just." He put his hand to his forehead, flustered. "I wasn't expecting that. It's weird. I guess, I'm sorry. I just didn't think of that. See? I don't think about that. I haven't thought about it since . . . since the accident. I'm sorry."

His smile was long gone and in its place was confusion and conflict. I took his hand and let out a breath that hopefully was a show of patience. "Hey, don't apologise. It'll happen when you're ready."

His gaze darted between my eyes. "What if it doesn't? What if it never happens?"

"Then it doesn't."

"Would you miss it?" he asked, his gaze imploring. "Do you miss it already? God, you do. You said your dick doesn't understand."

"Justin, baby, listen." I turned on the couch to face him more squarely and I held his hand in both of mine. "In the last four years we had a lot of sex. Like, a lot. We were very . . . physical, and before your accident I would have said that, yes, sex was important. But I know different now. It's not important. Not anymore. What's important is that you're alive, for one thing. Because you almost weren't. And secondly, that you're healthy and happy. Sex is just one aspect, and it's not compulsory. If we could never have sex again, for some medical reason, I'd still love you. I'd still be with you. What kind of arsehole would I be if I broke up with you because we couldn't have sex?"

He sighed and put his head on my shoulder, then sidled in a little closer, and when I put my arm around him, he sighed again. "I want to. I mean, I want to have sex again. I want to want it. I want to do that, with you."

I rubbed his back. "When you're ready, baby. There's no rush."

"Maybe now I know it's something I *can* think about, I'll start thinking about it."

I chuckled and kissed the side of his head. "Maybe. Don't stress about it, Juss. If it happens, it happens."

"I like kissing you though," he murmured. "A lot. I like it a lot."

"I like it too."

"Even though your dick doesn't understand?"

I snorted. "My dick will get over it."

He sat up and looked at me. "This is a totally normal conversation to be having, right?"

I laughed. "One hundred per cent."

He looked at me for a long moment. "Thank you. For not getting mad or making me feel bad. I'm trying to find myself and find my feet. It's confusing and it's not fair, to either of us, but you're really great, Dallas. I honestly don't know where I'd be without you."

I could tell by his voice and by how slow he spoke that he was getting tired. I gently booped him on the nose with my finger. "You're really great too, Juss. And I don't know where I'd be without you either."

He smiled and blushed, looking down at his lap. "So, uh, so we used to have a lot of sex?"

I laughed again. Most days, for the all the years we've been together. I didn't say that though. "Uh, yeah."

"I remember that couch and the blue bed," he whispered. He shook his head and licked his lips. "Was it like that all the time?"

I nodded. "Pretty much."

He chuckled and chewed on his bottom lip. Lord, help me, he had no idea how seductive that was . . . Then he took out his phone. "What are you doing?" I asked.

"I'm gonna put a reminder," he said. "Every hour, think about sex. If I need to retrain my brain, I should start tonight."

I barked out a laugh. "You always were dedicated."

He slumped against the back of the couch, smiling but tired. He threaded his fingers with mine. "Thank you."

"You're very welcome." I stood up, and still holding his hand, I helped him to his feet. "Let's get you to bed."

He fell into me, very deliberately, pressing his front to mine. He slipped his arms around me and snuggled his head into my neck. "Hug first."

I would never say no to that. I hugged him tight and relished his warmth. Holding him in my arms was soul-fixing. It felt good to comfort him and protect him, and it felt amazing to have that in return.

"Wish I wasn't always tired," he mumbled.

I pulled back and cupped his face. "I know you probably don't see it, but you're getting better every day. Two weeks ago you would've been in bed hours ago." I kissed him softly. "Every day is a step forward, baby. We don't need to run. Just a step a day, that's all."

Justin put his hand to my face and pulled me down for another kiss before putting his forehead to my chin. "I don't know what I ever did four years ago to deserve you, but I'm so thankful for you."

"I know you are. But thank you for telling me." I took his arm. "Come on. Let's go to bed."

While he used the bathroom, I turned everything off and locked up, and after brushing my teeth, I slid into bed beside him. As always, he melded himself into me and I welcomed the embrace.

I wasn't exactly tired, but I wasn't missing this. Not for anything. But sure enough, with his weight and his heat and that contented, peaceful feeling, I was soon drifting off.

Juss stirred a bit during the night but he stayed asleep, and he clung to me more than usual. I assumed it was all the talk about sex and his uncertainty surrounding his lack of desire for it. He was confused as to why he hadn't even thought of it, let alone wanted it. I was fairly certain it would come back to him when he was ready.

I meant what I'd said to him earlier. Sex wasn't compulsory for me. It wasn't a critical component of a relationship to me. I loved the man, not his body. Well, my heart loved the man. My dick, on the other hand, loved his body.

I woke up to find myself spooning him, though he was awake. He wiggled against me for a moment, then stopped before he peeled himself away from me and sat up, taking most of the blankets with him. "Jesus," he mumbled.

I opened my eyes to find him staring at . . . well, at my dick.

"Fucking hell, Dallas," he said. "Your dick is huge. Should I . . . I dunno, should I get it its own pillow?"

I snorted and scrubbed my hands over my face. "Good morning."

"It's huge." He was still staring at my dick. "I mean, it

explains a lot, like why I spent four years with a Bulldogs supporter."

I barked out a laugh and readjusted my very-hard cock. I was only wearing briefs—probably not a great idea, but I'd woken up every day before him, so it had never been an issue before. "Sorry," I croaked. "I'm normally up by now."

"You are," he said, nodding toward my dick.

I wasn't sure what to say to that. He was still staring at it. Was he uncomfortable? "I'll go have a shower," I said, sitting up. "Wanna make some coffee?"

He didn't answer, and when I looked at his face, he was staring at the blankets now pooled at my hips. "I want to watch."

Watch? What the . . . ?

"Watch me do what? Shower?"

"No. Well, sure, yeah, that too. Probably. But I mean . . . I want to watch . . ." He swallowed hard. "God, I can't believe I'm going to say this. I want to watch you get your-self off."

Christ.

"You want me to jerk off? Now?"

He nodded woodenly and met my eyes. "Yeah." He licked his lips and let out a shaky breath.

Fucking hell. He was dead serious. Could I jerk off in front of him? We'd certainly done more than that before, and my dick was most definitely keen. "Um." I cleared my throat and gave myself a squeeze. "Just like this?"

He propped the pillows up against the headboard behind me, then moved to the end of the bed on his side. Okay then, we were doing this. I shuffled up and leaned against the pillows, my legs spread. My briefs were barely restraining my cock and I pulled it free. I didn't need to be too comfortable; this was going to be over in seconds.

Justin's mouth was open, his eyes fixated and dark. He was breathing hard, and his gaze felt like hands on my body.

I fisted the base of my cock and stroked, sliding up to the tip and smearing the precome that was leaking from the slit. As soon as I twisted my palm over the head, a stab of bliss hit me, so I did it again, and again, and my balls drew up tight. I worked my hand up and down the shaft and it was too much. There was no going back, I was too far gone.

"Fuck, Juss. I'm gonna come so quick."

He was almost panting, and he nodded. "Do it. I want to see it."

Oh God.

My orgasm burned hot and fast, trailing a line of fire from the base of my spine, deep in my balls. It scorched hot and heavenly and spilled onto my belly. I groaned through my release, writhing with the pleasure of it.

"Fuck," Juss whispered.

I could barely open my eyes, and I laughed through my post-orgasmic haze. "You liked that?"

"That was hot as hell," he said, giving his dick a squeeze, and he groaned.

"Did you want to do the same?" I asked, nodding to the bulge in his boxers.

He looked down at his crotch and then at me. "Um, no, I'm good, thanks. I mean, I don't need . . . that. I just wanted to see you. And it was sexy. Christ. But I'm not . . ."

"You don't need to do anything until you're ready," I said. "But I probably should have a shower."

He nodded quickly, and his unease and awkwardness made me a little sad. I figured the best thing for me to do was clean up and get rid of the evidence currently drying on my belly. A quick shower later, I followed my nose to the kitchen. Justin had made coffee and toast, and he offered me a full cup.

"Thanks," I said, taking it from him.

Keeping his gaze averted, he slid the plate with toast over. "I'll just . . . I'm gonna take a shower too. I won't be long."

Before I could swallow my mouthful of coffee, he was gone. Goddammit. I didn't want things to be awkward between us. This was why he wasn't ready for sex. Sure, his body had liked what he'd watched, but his mind wasn't ready for the next step. I sighed and finished my breakfast before cleaning up, and it wasn't long until Justin reappeared freshly showered and dressed. He was wearing grey tracksuit pants and a hoodie, and he was holding a pair of socks and headed straight for the couch. "We still going shopping?" he asked. He pulled his left sock on easily enough, but his right was always a bit trickier, and I wasn't sure if it just took a little longer than necessary or if he was avoiding looking at me.

I sat at the other end of the couch and pulled my sneakers on. "You sure you're up for the supermarket?" It had been my idea but he was excited to go. It'd been weeks since he'd really been anywhere, and when I'd mentioned needing to grab a few groceries, he was keen to come along.

He shot me a quick look and gave a tight smile before reaching for his sneakers. "Oh yeah, for sure. I want to. Pretty lame when the supermarket is my social outing."

"It's not lame. This way you get to choose which ice cream flavour we get."

He got his left shoe on okay, but he struggled a bit with his right. I knelt in front of him and helped slide his heel into his sneaker and quickly tied his laces. It certainly wasn't the first time I'd helped him with shoes or getting dressed, but he seemed a little pissed that I was helping him now. Or maybe it was because I was on the floor between his knees . . .

I got to my feet and helped him stand, and he smiled and mumbled his thanks, but he was definitely uncomfortable. And, like he knew I was about to bring it up, he gave me a smile. "We ready to go? If we leave it too late, I'll need a nap in the soup aisle."

Okay then, he clearly wasn't ready to talk about it. And who knew, maybe he just needed some time to get his head around it and to process his newfound sexual awareness. So we threw his scooter in the back of the ute and headed to the local Coles. It was good to see him smile as we went around each section. He chose the fruit and veggies while I grabbed the bread, but then we took our time going up and down each aisle.

Most of it was mundane stuff and food and packaging he was very familiar with, but there were a few things he had to look at twice. Things that were new in the last five years, some things he had no recollection of eating, a lot of changed packaging, and even the layout of the supermarket had changed. There were so many small changes that I hadn't even considered until he'd commented.

I put a packet of our favourite taco kits in the trolley. "Have I eaten that before?" he asked. "Do I like that kind of pasta? Where've the eggs gone? They sell clothes now?"

But I appreciated his questions. It was proof to me he was getting better, that his mind was clearing, that his cognitive recognition was improving.

"Oh my God, Snickers ice creams are a thing now?" he asked, staring at the freezer.

I just laughed and threw a pack in the trolley.

headed for the checkout and made our way home. The trip itself didn't take us long and it wasn't overly strenuous, but it was a great test for Justin. And sure enough, by the time we got home, he was tired.

I carted all the bags up the stairs and he put things away, but he was fighting every long blink and shaking his head trying to stay awake. "Hey, why don't you go get on the couch and find us something to watch. I'll finish up here and—"

"I'm fine," he replied sharply.

Which was basically Exhibit A of him not being fine.

"Okay," I said, trying to smooth it over. I left the bag of dry goods for him and began putting Squish's food in the bottom of the pantry.

"I can help you with the damn groceries, Dallas," he ‌pped. "I'm not completely useless."

‌ slid the last can of cat food in, stood, and faced him, ‌ d at his outburst. "I know you're not, Juss. You're far ‌eless."

‌, I couldn't get my shoe on earlier, so that was ‌ing useless."

‌ e?" I was lost for a moment. "You couldn't get ‌ ecause you had surgery on your shattered leg ‌ as broken in two places."

‌ ed to remind me!"

‌less, Justin. That's—"

‌y reality? Because apparently there's a ‌"

‌ow?" he ‌ rget it. Put the . . ." He looked at ‌ u put them away."

‌, then we ‌ as he walked to the bedroom, ‌ him. I stood there, stunned.

What the fuck was that about? His struggle to find the right word was a clear sign he was tired, and maybe going to the supermarket had been too much. Though I was certain it was the sex-incident this morning that had him so off-kilter.

His mind was obviously working overtime trying to figure shit out, and he was tired, and yeah, the doctors had said to expect mood swings. I knew this wasn't about me. This was about Justin and his recovery, both physical and mental.

But fucking hell . . . It hurt me too.

Not knowing what else to do, I put the groceries away. He clearly needed some space and some sleep, so I left him to it and went downstairs. I checked my emails and wasn't surprised to find the insurance or workers' comp people hadn't replied. Not that I expected them to on a Sunday, but I was fast losing patience and it added to my frustration and stress levels.

I resisted throwing my laptop across my office. Barely.

I stood in my office at a loss of what to do next. Every pressure, every worry, was bearing down on me, and I wasn't sure how much more I could take. I wanted to punch something, to vent the anger, the blame.

I wanted to blame something for this whole fucking mess, but there was nothing, no one. It wasn't anyone's fault. It was just what life threw at me. *Here, Dallas, have some more fucking shit. You can handle it.*

Well, life. Guess what? I'm beginning to think I can't.

If I had a limit, I was pretty sure I'd found it.

Justin yelling at me was the cherry on top of a whole mountain of clusterfuck. And him yelling wasn't his fault either. He couldn't help it.

I hated that it was going to come down to money. Maybe Justin was right about selling his bike. Not that I'd sell *his* bike, but I could sell mine, or my ute. I'd just have to buy something cheaper to get us from A to B. He still had doctor appointments we needed to get to, and he wasn't ready to be on the back of a bike.

I had a rough idea what the market value would be for a ute like mine, and it would get us out of trouble for a little while.

Christ.

It really was something I was going to have to think about this week. If I didn't get some money coming in soon, selling some stuff might be my only option.

I couldn't bear to think about it anymore. I needed to do something with my hands to get my mind off my freaking money troubles, so I rifled through the cleaning cupboard and found a half-used, long-forgotten bottle of window cleaner and a roll of paper towel. I cleaned every window I could reach, then found the old ladder from the storeroom for the windows I couldn't. I doubted some of those windows had ever been cleaned.

It felt good to scrub the shit out of them; using physical strength was great for venting frustration. Using mindless elbow grease was a much-needed distraction. I lost track of time and was working up a sweat scrubbing the last window when I thought I heard something . . .

Then I heard it again.

"Dallas!"

I was down that ladder and sprinting up the back stairs as fast as I could. I burst inside the flat. "Justin?"

He replied with a sob and I raced into the bedroom. He was sitting up in bed with tears streaming down his face. "You were gone," he cried, his chest heaving. "You left me."

I sat on the edge of the bed beside him and pulled him against me, my heart hammering, trying to catch my breath.

"I'm here, baby. I was just downstairs. I'll never leave you, I promise."

"I can't do this without you. I thought you'd left me, and I had a nightmare and you weren't here."

I rubbed his back to soothe him. "Oh, baby. I'll never leave you."

"I'm sorry," he mumbled. He pulled away and looked at me, his eyes so full of sadness. "For what I said. I'm sorry. I don't know why I was horrible to you."

"It's okay. You were tired."

"It's not okay. I'm sorry."

I wiped his tears and pushed his hair back. "Baby, I forgive you."

Which of course set off another wave of tears. "I want to be normal for you," he sobbed. "I want to be what you need, but I don't know if I can."

"Juss, you are normal," I replied, not really knowing what normal was anyway. "You're perfect, just the way you are. You don't need to try to be anything."

He searched my eyes; his bottom lip trembled. "I want to have sex with you, but I don't know if I can."

Wait, what?

My mind spun from my own troubles, but there it was. The truth about what he was so stressed about.

"Juss, you don't have to worry about that."

"I want to. And this morning in bed, you wanted it too. What you did was so hot. And my body wanted it, but my brain couldn't . . . not yet. I don't know why."

"Because you're not ready, that's why. And baby, that's okay."

"You're not mad?"

"Mad? Why would I be mad?"

"You wanted me to . . . do what you did." He got all teary again. "In bed."

"No, baby. I just asked if you wanted to, that's all. I didn't mean you had to or that I wanted you to. I just . . ." I sighed. "I'm sorry if I made you feel that way. That wasn't my intention."

"I don't want to disappoint you. I want to be with you. I want to make you happy," he said, scrubbing at his face.

"You do make me happy," I whispered. "You could never disappoint me."

He gave me the most adorable puppy dog eyes. "I was horrible to you."

I smiled and cupped his face. "You weren't horrible. Juss, you couldn't be horrible if you tried." I kissed his forehead. "We had a little fight, that's all. Just a misunderstanding. You were tired, and anyway, I like putting the groceries away."

That earned me a small, brief smile. "I'm sorry."

"I know you are." I studied him for a second. "You had a nightmare?"

He frowned and gave a small nod. "Because you weren't here. I called out to you but you didn't answer and I called out again, but . . ." He swallowed hard. "I remembered the look on your face before I walked out and I thought, fuck, I'd really done it this time. I thought you'd left me, and I wouldn't have blamed you. I can't do this without you."

I crawled over his legs and lay down in the middle of the bed and pulled him in for a proper hug. I could hold him better this way. "I was just downstairs, cleaning. I lost track of time, I'm sorry you were scared."

He sighed, and with his head on my chest, I held him tighter. "You're a bit hot and sweaty."

I snorted. "Sorry."

"No, I like it." He very slowly rubbed his face along my chest. "You smell good."

I sighed, and for a few unspoken minutes, we just lay there while I rubbed his back. "Feel better now?" I asked.

"Yeah. I meant what I said, though. I can't do this without you."

I kissed the top of his head. "Just as well you don't have to."

"Dallas," he whispered. "I want to . . . start doing things with you. Physical things. Sexual things. Because my body is, well, my body says yes."

"But your mind says no."

"My brain is messed up."

I chuckled. "No it's not, Juss. Your brain is recovering. It'll happen when you're ready. Just be patient."

"How long will it take?"

"I don't know. How about you talk about it with Doctor Chang this week? She knows so much more than me."

He sighed and lifted his head up off my chest so he could see my face. "I'm sorry about this morning. I feel bad."

"You don't have to feel bad," I murmured. I trailed my fingers through the hair at his temple. "Just talk to me next time, okay? About anything. You can ask me anything you want to know."

"Can I ask you something now?"

"Sure."

"Can you kiss me?" He was so genuinely nervous, it was cute. Like I'd ever say no to that. "I just want to feel close to you and I really like kissing. Is that too much to ask?"

I leaned in and captured his mouth with mine and rolled us onto our sides. I had to be careful of his body: his arm, his leg, his head. But if I cradled him, held him close, and wrapped him up in my arms, it was almost impossible to hurt him.

He melted into me and opened his mouth, deepening the kiss. Our bodies aligned and he slid his arm around my back, but we never pushed to take it any further. That's not what this was. This wasn't about me pushing to see how far he'd let me go or for him to see how far he wanted to go. This was purely a reconnect, an act of intimacy, of tenderness, between two men in love.

He did love me; I knew he did. He'd said before I made it too easy for him to love me, and I took that as a declaration.

This was about Justin feeling some kind of normalcy. There had been so much taken from him, so much disconnection. If kissing made him feel in control or if he was taking back something that was stolen from him—or even if he did it because it made him feel good—then I would kiss him all day long.

Or I'd kiss him until my stomach growled so loud it made him laugh.

"Is that lunchtime?" he asked, smiling against my lips.

"Yeah, probably later than that, actually."

He frowned. "I kinda messed up our whole day, didn't I?"

"Not at all."

"You have gorgeous eyes," he murmured, his gaze darting back and forth. He put his hand to my face. "And I feel like I know your eyes. They're familiar, like we've lain like this hundreds of times."

That made me smile. "Well, I never counted."

"I know your eyes," he whispered again. "I always liked them, didn't I?"

I kissed him, soft and warm. "Yes you did."

"They're a grey-hazel that I've never seen anywhere else. And it's not even the colour, but it's what's in them, what's behind them." His gaze intensified as he studied me. "They tell me all the things you don't say."

Why was that both scary and heartening? "What's that?"

"Honesty, and the truth. You see me, and you love me."

"I do."

"I know. And I'm so grateful for you."

"I never was much good at hiding anything from you."

My stomach growled again and he smiled. "Including when you need food. We should feed you."

So we went to the kitchen and made sandwiches and we stood leaning against the kitchen counter as we ate. I hadn't realised just how hungry I was until I had food in front of me. I shoved half my sandwich into my mouth and Justin laughed at me as I struggled to chew it. "What?" I managed to ask around the food, trying to not laugh.

He smiled at me for a long moment, his sandwich in his hand. "I love you."

I was so stunned I almost couldn't swallow.

He took a small bite, smiling as he chewed. "It's true, I do. I think some part of me knows I always have. But when I woke up and you weren't here, I realised I don't just need you. I realised that I love you. My heart never forgot you, Dallas. I just thought you should know."

I threw my arms around him in a fierce hug. "Oh my God, Juss."

He laughed, then mumbled into my chest, "You're crushing my sandwich."

I laughed and let him go, planting a kiss on his lips, his cheek, his temple. "I love you too."

CHAPTER NINE

DOCTOR CHANG WELCOMED us into her office. "How are you both?" she asked. "Justin, you look great!"

He sat in one of the two seats opposite her desk; I took the other. "Oh, thanks."

"No scooter today?"

"No, it's in the ute but I thought I'd walk. I'll need a nap when I get home, but it's nice not to need it all the time."

She smiled. "And how's your week been? Have you had any other memories or other breakthroughs?"

"Memories, yes. Flashes of some, full memories of others."

"That's great! Were they happy memories?"

He glanced at me and blushed. "Well, yeah. Intimate ones."

"Oh." Her smile twisted, amused. "And how did that make you feel?"

"Um." He barked out a laugh and reached for my hand. "Loved. It made me feel loved. But more than that, I remember how I felt. The memory wasn't . . . empty, like a photo of things I didn't remember. I was there, I remember being there, what we did, how it felt." He put his free hand to his heart. "I remember it."

"The correlation between memory and emotion is very strong," Doctor Chang said. "Experiencing something first-hand and remembering it help provide a connection between memory and self, who you are."

Justin nodded. "I've had other memories, but this one was . . . I mean, they all mean something, but this one meant the most."

"Because of the emotional connection." Doctor Chang smiled proudly at Justin, then turned her attention to me. "And Dallas, how was your week?"

I squeezed Juss' hand. "We had some ups and downs. More ups than downs, but we ended on a high."

"What were the lows?"

"I was an idiot," Juss answered.

I laughed. "No you weren't. He wasn't," I told Doctor Chang. "He was tired and overwhelmed and a bit scared about what everything meant. It was totally understandable, and we talked about it until he felt better."

She frowned. "Scared? Justin, what were you scared about?"

He gave me another look and his grip on my hand was bone-crunching. "Sex. I hadn't thought about sex, not really. Or, not even once. Since the accident. And I mean, how could I not think about it?" He made a face. "Being reminded that sex was even a thing that I did was like being told I used to speak another language before the accident, only I couldn't remember it. All awareness of it was gone. I mean I knew it was a thing, but I hadn't thought about actually doing it."

"Loss of libido is not uncommon," the doc said gently.

"It's not that I don't want to have sex. Now that I've

remembered it, it's just . . . I do want to. I think. God, I dunno." Justin met my eyes. "And Dallas was really good about it. I mean, Dallas is good about everything. But he was patient and told me not to worry about it until I was ready and there was no rush. But then I worried that there was something wrong with me." He looked back to the doc then. "Is there? Something wrong with me?"

"Not at all, Justin," she replied. "It's very common."

"I want to try," he admitted. "And my body is like an RC 390 but my brain is the handbrake, ya know?" He made a face. "Sorry, an RC 390 is fast."

She smiled at that. "You think something's holding you back?"

"You mean my broken brain?"

"Your brain's not broken, Juss," I offered.

"So why is my brain being stupid? Why do I freak out at the thought of it?"

That was something I couldn't answer. I looked to the doctor. She smiled gently and said, "Our minds put up warnings when it senses danger. It's a defence mechanism."

"Danger?" Justin asked.

"Fear," she replied. "Are you afraid of something?"

Justin's eyes flashed and his grip on my hand pulsed. She'd hit the nail right on the head, and Justin looked panicked. God, was this something he wanted to discuss in private? I didn't want him to be uncomfortable.

"Do you want me to wait outside?" I asked.

"No," he shot back quickly, pulling my hand to his body as if to keep me close. "Please stay."

"Okay," I murmured, nodding.

He swallowed hard and took a second before he looked back at Doctor Chang. "I guess, yeah. And I don't know why."

"You don't know why, what?" she asked patiently.

"I don't know why I'm scared. I shouldn't be. I've done it before."

"What are you scared of?" I asked.

Justin seemed stuck, unable to answer, so Doctor Chang did. "After a traumatic experience, where someone has experienced significant levels of pain, it's not uncommon for that person to reject any scenario where they may experience any kind of pain again."

What? Pain? Oh God . . .

"Justin," I breathed. "I would never hurt you."

His eyes darted to mine, full of fear and honesty. "I know. It's why it doesn't make sense."

"It does make sense," Doctor Chang said. "And it's completely justified. What you went through was a significant ordeal, where you spent many weeks in all kinds of pain. And you still have pain, yes?"

He nodded. "My leg. My arm doesn't hurt much unless I wrench it or overuse it."

"And your head?"

He slow blinked as though even the mention of his headaches made his head hurt. "My head hurts most days. The meds help."

"Is the severity of the pain getting less?" she asked.

"I think so," he replied. "I mean, yeah. I guess."

She talked him through some techniques and recognition signals and basically suggested that if it was something he really wanted to do, he use the small steps system. Proceed slowly and stop when it became too much, and of course, to practise patience and be open with how we both felt.

But Justin had done the right thing by admitting his fear and it was the first step, she said, and she was happy that we were talking about it. A lot of couples didn't and she said it showed how much we cared for each other. "There's a very strong bond between you," she said as our meeting finished.

"I love him," Justin said, his cheeks a rich pink. He glanced to me and laughed, his fingers laced with mine. "I always did, I think. Even when he was sitting by my bed in hospital and I wasn't sure who he was, I never wanted him to leave. His visits were the highlight of every day, and when I had to leave the hospital and go home, I wanted to go with him. I can't tell you why, apart from the fact he made me feel safe, but I honestly think my heart knew."

I would have kissed him if we weren't in a doctor's office. "I love you too, Juss. Always have, always will."

Juss smiled all shy-like and he breathed out a laugh. "Always have, always will," he repeated.

For a brief moment, I think we both forgot we were sitting across from Doctor Chang. When I looked over, she was smiling at us, her whole face soft. "You two just kill me."

Justin promised to keep up his physio and to write any new developments in his journal and, of course, not to overdo anything, and with another promise to see her again next week, we were on our way.

Halfway home and Justin still hadn't said anything. "You okay?" I asked.

He turned and gave me a tired smile. "Yeah. Feel good, actually. Better now we've talked to her."

"I'm glad. I feel better too. Relieved, I think."

"Yeah." He nodded. "You know how she told me to go slow, with sex, and see what I'm comfortable with?"

"Yeah? What about it?"

"What do you think she meant by go slow?"

"Oh, well . . . I think she meant we should start by

making out, and as you get more comfortable, progress from there, but just a step at a time, that kind of thing."

He smirked. "Well, I think we should try that."

"You do?"

"Yep. It's technically a doctor's order."

I laughed. "True. It was."

He grinned. "Making out. In bed. This afternoon."

"Is that right?"

"Or on the couch. I can't decide."

I laughed again. "Less pressure on the couch," I suggested, thinking the idea of making out in our bed might be too much, that it may lead to sex.

He stared at me. "I can remember what we did on that couch on our weekend away, remember? At Hallidays? There was a leather couch and I can remember what you did to me on it." Then his bottom lip drew down. "I also remember what we did in the bed . . . God, is there anywhere we haven't had sex?"

I snorted. "Um . . ."

"The bathroom?"

I made a face.

"God. The kitchen?"

I made another face.

"Christ. The dining table? You know what? Don't answer that. Did we have sex everywhere?"

"Pretty much."

He sighed. "Well, maybe we should start with the couch."

I took his hand and brought it up to my lips, kissing his knuckles. "I'm sure we'll figure it out."

"Have you gotta work today?"

"Yeah."

"Shame."

I groaned. "You're cruel."

He laughed. "I'm sorry. I shouldn't tease." Then he turned serious. "Honestly though, I don't know if I can go through with it . . . Dallas, I'm sorry."

"Don't stress, and don't overthink it." I shrugged. "And anyway, you being a flirt and a tease is just like the old you, so I don't mind one bit."

"Yeah, but saying stuff is one thing. Going through with it is something else. God—"

"Hey," I said, kissing his knuckles again. "If you want to say something, then say it. I don't want you to censor yourself. I'm not gonna pressure you into sex because you say something flirty."

He sighed and sagged into his seat. "Thank you. It's weird. I have these moments where I feel completely normal, like nothing's different and there was no accident. As if my brain is playing some stupid before-and-after game. And I'll want to say something or do something, but then reality kicks in and I freeze because I don't know if it's something I'd do or say."

"Just be you, Juss," I said. "Whatever feels right."

I didn't want to say anything, but his recognition of these changes was huge. That he could recognise what was before and after, and adapt to suit, was a pretty big deal. Even though it confused him a little, his brain was changing gears and his thoughts were faster and clearer.

I pulled the ute around near the back stairs and Juss made his way up to the flat. If he worked at all today would depend on how he felt this afternoon. His doctor appointments always drained him. I followed him up and he plonked himself onto the sofa while I grabbed him a bottle of water and some crackers and grapes. I set them on the seat next to him and he pressed the button to activate the recliner. I settled the blanket over him and he gave me a tired smile.

"Thanks, babe," he murmured.

Babe? That term of endearment got me right in the heart and he was so cute, I just couldn't help it. I put my knee on the edge of the couch and leaned over him, kissing him. He responded immediately by deepening the kiss and I let him feel part of my weight on his body. When he put a hand on my waist and he moaned, it almost did me in. But I stopped and pulled back. "Get some sleep, baby," I murmured.

He made some disgruntled groan-sigh noise and I smiled as I stood up. His eyes drew down to my crotch where I was very aware of my arousal. He clearly liked what he saw and he licked his lips.

It almost buckled my knees, but I let out a laugh instead, trying to get a hold of myself. *Small steps, Dallas.*

"I'll just be downstairs," I said, waiting until I was out of view before I readjusted myself.

"Now who's the tease?" he mumbled as I got to the door.

I laughed as I bounded down the stairs and was still smiling when Sparra and Davo saw me. "Good day, I take it," Davo said, grinning at me.

"Yeah, not bad."

"Good to hear," he said. "Now get to work; we got two bikes to do this arvo."

I laughed and clapped his shoulder. "Sure thing, boss."

Sparra laughed and the three of us hooked in and worked our backsides off to get it all done with time to spare. I got some admin stuff done in the few minutes the boys were finishing up, checked my bank account and saw one client's late payments had come through, which meant I could pay wages without having to dip into my credit card, and maybe put off selling my ute for another week. It felt like a game of financial chess that I wasn't fit to play. I confirmed some more bookings for next week, thank God, and checked my emails for anything from the insurance company about the accident.

Still nothing.

Then I heard Davo and Sparra talking to someone, and a familiar voice and laugh filtered through the door. It was Justin. A few seconds later, he appeared in my office door-way, smiling. "Hey."

"Hey," I replied. "You get bored up there?"

"So bored." He walked in and parked his arse on my desk beside my chair. "Dinner's in the oven. I made shepherd's pie."

"Oh wow, thanks."

Davo cleared his throat at the door. "You, uh, you want me to lock you both in here again?"

I laughed. "Nah, I think we're good, thanks."

Justin was smiling too. "Actually, I wouldn't mind if you did."

Davo burst out laughing. "See you fellas tomorrow. I'll lock the gate behind us."

"Thanks, mate."

Sparra waved us off, leaving us alone. I closed my laptop and looked up where Juss still leaned against my desk. I put my hand on his thigh. "How're you feeling?"

"Pretty good. I slept for a while. Must have been tired."

"You want to help me close up?"

He smiled. "Yep."

So we made sure the gate was locked, then pulled the roller doors down, locking everything as we went. I helped Juss up the stairs, not that he needed it. He really was getting so much better. I doubted he'd be running up the stairs two at a time soon, if ever again, but at least each step wasn't a mountain.

Dinner was amazing, and he showed me what he'd added to his journal while we ate. Afterwards, I cleaned up the kitchen and told him to go get comfy and choose something for us to watch on TV. And when I was done and turned the lights off, he wasn't using the recliner part of the couch, but he was lying lengthways on the sofa. He had a cushion shoved under his head and was pointing the remote at the TV.

"I can tell you something that hasn't changed in five years," he said. "There is nothing to watch on TV."

He settled for some nature documentary and tossed the remote. "You comfortable there?" I asked. He looked comfy in his trackies and hoodie. "Where am I supposed to sit?"

"No sitting," he murmured, patting the couch in front of him. "Lie here with me."

"Oh."

"I was thinking you could kiss me again, like you did this afternoon."

"We've kissed before."

"But not with your body on top of mine." He shuffled around a bit so he was on his back and not on his side so much.

Oh Christ. "You want me to lie on top of you?"

"Yeah. You know, the doctor said we should."

I laughed. "She did."

"You'll just need to watch my leg," he said. His right leg was bent at the knee and pressed against the back of the couch, which, yes, kept it out of the way, but it meant if I lay on him, I'd be between his legs.

Hell yes . . .

"I'll be careful," I whispered. "And you can tell me to stop at any time. If I hurt you, like if I accidently bump your leg or your arm, tell me."

"I will." He held out his hand to me.

So, very carefully, I put a knee on the couch and gently lowered myself on top of him. I was between his legs, holding my weight on my arms, but my hips were aligned with his. There was no way he couldn't feel my semi-hard dick. "How's that feel?"

He nodded quickly. "Really good."

I ghosted my lips over his, slow and tender, and he lifted his head to chase my mouth. It made me smile. "Small steps, baby."

"Shut up and kiss me."

I barked out a laugh because that was such a Justin thing to say. But I gave him what he wanted. I kissed him hard, opening his lips with mine, tasting his tongue and sucking it into my mouth.

He groaned and rolled his hips, then he gasped.

I stopped and pulled back. "You okay?"

He nodded, breathless. His cheeks were flushed and his pupils were blown. "Yeah. That was hot."

I kissed him again, slower this time, less urgent. He slid his hand under my shirt and up my back and it took every ounce of self-control not to lift his leg up, buck my hips, and drive into him.

I shuddered with restraint and he smiled into our kiss. "You like that?" he asked.

I put my hand to the side of his face, thumbing his hair back. "I like everything we're doing right now."

"Me too. This feels . . . right."

That earned him another kiss, then another, and we settled into a lazy make-out session. There was no hurried groping, no hurtling toward getting each other off. It was languid and dreamy. I could feel his erection against mine, but we simply revelled in the closeness, the intimacy.

I didn't even want to come. I just wanted to ride out this incredible high for as long as possible. And when the kissing ran its course, we simply held each other and traded soft touches and smiles until he was dozing off.

"We should get you to bed," I whispered.

"You too," he mumbled, his eyes still closed.

"Of course."

He was clingy; even when we brushed our teeth, he wanted to be touching me, and when we climbed into bed, he nestled right in against me. He rested his head on my shoulder, his warm breath on my neck. He'd always been my very own cuddly koala in the way he clung to me, and I pulled him even closer. I kissed the side of his head. "I love you, Juss."

"Love you too," he mumbled.

I smiled into the darkness and held him just that little bit tighter.

CHAPTER TEN

"CHRIST, YOU HAVE A REALLY BIG DICK."

I opened my eyes and barked out a laugh. Justin was sitting up in bed, the blankets pooled at his hips, and he was staring at the bulge in my briefs. "Good morning," I replied, my voice croaking. "Sleep okay?"

"Mm, guess."

"What time is it?"

"Dunno."

I rolled over and checked my phone. "Six thirty."

He was still looking at my dick.

"Juss, you okay?"

His eyes darted to mine. "Yeah. I'm fine."

But he wasn't. This seemed more than his usual not-a-morning-person thing. His brain was overthinking again.

I pulled the blanket up to cover my crotch. "Want me to make eggs on toast for brekky?"

His gaze darted to mine again, and he seemed to snap out of his own head. "Um. Yeah. I think. I dunno. Whatever you think."

I reached over and rubbed his back. "Everything okay,

Juss? If you'd rather I slept in some shorts or trackies, I can. It's no problem."

"No, I just . . ." He swallowed hard. "I like it. I'm just not . . ."

"Not what?"

"I'm not sure what I'm supposed to do?"

"About what? My dick? You're not supposed to do anything."

"Not yours . . . I mean, yours is . . ." He let out a breath. "Yours is fucking hot. But mine . . ."

"Yours? Juss, what's wrong? Is something wrong?"

"No." He scrubbed his hands over his face. "I, um, I had a dream that we were . . ." He cringed. "I woke up with a hard-on, and I dunno . . . what the hell do I do with it? I mean, I know what I can do with it. Ugh God, this is embarrassing."

I almost laughed with relief but managed to offer a smile instead. "Baby, you can do whatever you want. If you want to ignore it, then ignore it. If you want to jerk off, then do that. There's no judgement here."

"Really?"

"Yeah, really. Believe me, I've jerked off in the shower a lot since I started sleeping in here with you these last few weeks."

"You have?"

"Sure. Like I told you before, my head and my heart understand what's going on, but my dick didn't get the memo."

He almost smiled, but that line between his eyebrows was back. He studied the doona for a bit. "I'll just go have a shower," he said, then stopped. "Not to . . . jerk off. Just to shower. God, that's not what I meant."

I chuckled. "It's fine, baby. I'll go make a start on breakfast."

I rolled out of bed and filled the kettle before switching it on, then pulled the eggs out of the fridge when Justin walked out of the bathroom. He was still wearing his boxers; his hair was still a mess from sleep. He looked both worried and determined.

"Juss, what is it? Is something wrong with the shower?"

"Not the shower, no." He put his hand over his eyes, and with a frustrated groan, he sagged and then gripped his dick. "It won't go away. I thought maybe you'd like to help me . . ."

Hell fucking yes, I would.

After sliding the eggs onto the kitchen bench, I took his hand and led him to the couch. Once he sat in the middle seat, I pressed the button for the recliner to come up and gently lifted his right leg so it was resting on the recliner, his left foot still on the floor.

I knelt between his legs. "Comfy?"

He nodded.

"Tell me if you need me to stop, at any time, and I'll stop."

He nodded again, but his eyes were darker, his lips were parted.

God, he was so sexy.

I palmed his dick first, and yeah, he was rock hard. He pushed his hips up at the touch, desperate for friction. "I need . . ."

I pulled the front of his boxers down and freed his cock. It thwacked against his belly, red and swollen, leaking precome. It looked painfully hard. I gripped his shaft and he groaned.

"Feel okay?" I asked.

He nodded again. "Need to come, Dallas."

I leaned in and licked his shaft from base to tip and he hissed, but he raised his hips again, desperate. So I sucked him into my mouth and tongued the head before taking him in as far as I could. I sucked him good and hard until he arched, and his cock pulsed and shot his load into my mouth.

He tasted familiar and wonderful, and I drank, sucking and licking him clean. He writhed with the pleasure of it, then sagged when it was over. I was pretty sure his muscles, particularly in his leg, weren't used to that kind of strain.

"How are you feeling now?"

He replied with a snort and a laugh.

"Okay, smiley. That's gonna wear off in a minute." I got to my feet and gently pulled him to his. "Let's get you into a hot shower."

He let me lead him to the bathroom, let me undress him, reminding me almost of the early days after his accident. There were no thought processes, just blind obedience. But this time it was a little different; he was just blissed out. I turned the water on and held his arm. "You okay?"

He nodded. "Yeah. I feel . . . really good."

"I'm glad. Okay, water's hot enough. Hop in."

"You too," he replied, taking my hand. "You can shower with me."

"Um . . ." I hesitated.

"I could fall," he said.

I met his gaze, trying to see if he was joking or not.

"Don't want me to fall, do you?" he added with the hint of a smirk.

"The shower's not real big."

"Then we better stand close," he said. He stepped into

the shower and held his hand out. "You're getting water on the floor."

I rolled my eyes and slid my pants down before following him into the shower. There wasn't much room at all, so I pressed my back against the tiles. He stood with his head under the spray, letting the hot water course over his neck and shoulders for a long moment before he handed me the soap. "Do my back?" he asked, throwing me a dirty smirk as he turned his back to me.

I soaped him up, good and proper. His back, his shoulders, his arms, his arse. Fuck, his arse was beautiful.

When he turned around, his eyes went straight to my now very erect cock. He licked his lips. "Fuck, Dallas." He took the soap from me and washed my chest, my stomach. But then he ditched the soap and took my hand, wrapping my fingers around my dick and he helped pump me a few times. "I want to watch you come."

And the combination of last night and all that making out, waking up with a hard-on, then giving him head on the couch and being naked with him in the shower had me close to the edge in no time.

No, he wasn't ready to be the one who jerked me off, let alone suck me—not that he could in a shower anyway, not with his leg—but this was a big step for him. And knowing he was taking this step for me . . .

I tweaked my nipple as I stroked myself, then reached down to my balls. "Oh, fuck," I mumbled. The hot water, the steam, Justin standing there, watching me like he wanted to devour me.

I came so hard the room spun, and without any warning, Justin kissed me. His hands were in my hair, his tongue was in my mouth, and a wave of aftershocks barrelled through me as my come spilled between us.

"That was so fucking hot," he breathed. Then he traced a finger along the wing of my tattoo. "God, I love this ink, I love your body." He put his forehead to my collarbone and fell into a hug. "Love you too."

I was still in some post-orgasmic haze, but I managed to wrap my arms around him. "I love you, Juss. And I wish we could stay here forever but the water's gonna run cold soon."

He grumbled but we got out and dried off. "Need to use the bathroom," he said awkwardly, not meeting my gaze.

"Okay, I'll go start breakfast." I left him to it, quickly getting dressed before making coffee and cracking some eggs into a pan, all the while hoping his sudden downturn in mood as we dried off wasn't regret.

He took his time in the bathroom and getting dressed, so I was putting the toast on our plates on the table when he came back out. "Oh, hey," I began. "I made you scrambled—"

He cut my words off with a fierce hug. He slotted perfectly against me, holding me tight with his face pressed into my neck. "Oh!" I was stunned, to say the least. "You okay?"

He nodded against me. "I am now." He sighed but never made a move to let go. "Thank you, for not freaking out. For giving me what I needed when I didn't even know what I needed."

"You're welcome, baby. Was what we did okay? I thought you might have regretted what we did. Or that you weren't ready. It wasn't too much?"

"No, it was perfect." He pulled back. "I was a bit freaked out when I first woke up. I was so turned on, and that was really the first time I've felt like that since my accident. It wouldn't quit and I didn't know what to do. I wasn't ready to jerk off, I don't know why. But I thought you'd know what to do. And holy shit, did you ever."

I laughed at that. "I'm glad you're feeling better. And believe me, it was my absolute pleasure to help you with that problem."

He blushed. "It's so weird to talk about this stuff."

I kissed him softly, then pulled out his seat. "Sit down and have some brekky. We need to get downstairs. We've got a busy day at work today."

He smiled as he sat. "God, I'm starving. Thank you!"

I HUNG up the phone after taking another booking for next week, and Davo came into my office and sat down. "Jusso's helping Sparra with the full service on the Honda."

"Good. How's he going?" I'd been stuck in my office most of the morning and hadn't been on the workshop floor at all.

"He's handling it just fine. There's a change in him today," Davo said. "I dunno what, exactly, but he's almost like his old self. He's still moving slow with his leg and all, but his thinking is much clearer."

"Yeah. This morning . . . his brain told him he was actu-ally hungry. That's a good sign." I shrugged. There was no way I was telling him anything else that went on this morn-ing. "It's a real good sign. But we're still taking it one day at a time."

"Well, it's good to see. He was laughing out there before, so something's going right." He eyed me for a long second. "And by your smile, I reckon you agree."

I tried not to smile and failed. "Yeah, something's going right. We were so lucky. It could have been so much worse."

"He's getting better every day."

"He is."

"Good," Davo said with a grin. "He's been slacking off for too long."

I chuckled. "Did you come in here for any particular reason."

He nodded. "Yeah. To tell you it's lunchtime and pizza sounds good."

I laughed at him. "Yeah, righteo. Message received and understood."

Pizza ordered—and paid for on my credit card—I was just tidying up my desk when the phone rang again. "Muller's Mechanics, Dallas speaking."

"Uh, hello, Dallas," a man replied. He sounded older. "It's Jimmy Litchfield. We met at the hospital. I came in to see the young man, Justin, and you said I should call in a few weeks."

"Mr Litchfield. Yes, I remember you. I was there with Justin that day."

"How is he? Is he getting on okay? I worry about him."

"He's getting by okay, Mr Litchfield," I said. "Did you want to call in one day? I'm sure Justin'd like that."

"I sure would, if that'd be no trouble. Please, call me Jimmy."

"Just gimme one sec." I put the call on hold and went out in search of Juss. He was on his scooter, taking a spring off a suspension rig while Sparra was next to him unfastening an engine cap off the same bike. "Hey, Juss?" He looked up at me. "Do you remember the old guy, Jimmy Litchfield? He came to see you at the hospital."

Juss squinted one eye. "Uh, yeah. The truck driver, right?"

"Yeah." I held up the phone. "He wants to know if he

can call around sometime and see how you're getting on. Is that okay with you?"

Justin shrugged. "Sure. I guess."

I let Jimmy know it was all fine, that mornings were best, and he said he'd see us soon. The pizza arrived and we made real short work of that, and I didn't really give the phone call another thought until dinner time when Justin brought it up.

"What do you think the truck driver wants?" he asked.

"Honestly, I think he needs to know you're okay. I think he feels a lot of guilt, and knowing you're okay helps him with that."

Justin nodded slowly and pushed his salad around his plate. He hadn't slept for long this afternoon and I could see he was tired by his delayed speech and slow blinks. Clearly he had a lot on his mind. "He must be a nice guy."

"He seemed it," I replied. "When he came to the hospital, he was very upset. I thought he was genuine."

He nodded. "Says a lot that some stranger wants to visit but my own mother hasn't even called me."

I put my fork down and covered his hand with mine. "Oh, Juss. I'm sorry. Have you been thinking about her?"

He gave a slight shrug. "Mm. Bit hard not to. I mean, I didn't for a while when my brain was all foggy, but then I realised that she hasn't even called, so now I . . ." He sighed. "Now I know how she really feels, I guess."

I squeezed his hand. "Baby, I'm sorry. I'm sorry she's a horrible person. You deserve better."

"Did she call at all when I was in hospital?"

I shook my head. "No."

He frowned. "Becca said she told her and that her reaction was about as good as expected. She didn't say what was said, exactly, so I guess it was awful."

"Baby, she hasn't really been a part of your life since you came back to Newcastle. Not in the last five years. She certainly doesn't like me."

"Have you met her?"

I nodded. "Yeah. We went and saw her. You'd been back from Darwin for about six months and you hadn't seen her in two and a half years. We thought we'd see if she'd changed her attitude."

Something flashed in his eyes. "Was she mean to you?"

"Not directly. She was mean to you and disgusted that I wasn't a woman. She said some pretty horrible things."

His nostrils flared. His eyebrows knitted. "She never called me when I was in Darwin either. She hasn't really spoken to me since she found out I was gay. I dunno why I ever thought that'd change."

"Because you're a decent human being who never loses hope. And she's a terrible person and an even worse mother."

His gaze darted to mine and he smiled. "True. Still sucks, though."

"It does. I'm not denying that. My relationship with my family isn't much better. But we know what we're worth, and we know we deserve better." I put his hand to my face and kissed his palm. "We choose our own family, Juss."

"I'm so glad I found you," he whispered. "Twice."

I chuckled at that. "And I'm glad for the second chance."

And right on cue, Squish decided to yell at us from his bowl. "Yes, Squish. We're glad for you too," I said. "And for the record, there are biscuits in that bowl. You're not starving."

Justin laughed. "You know this . . ." He gestured

between us and then to the cat. "This was all I ever wanted."

"The family we choose, right?"

He laughed again but got teary as he nodded. "Yeah."

"Oh, baby," I said, sliding my chair over and pulling him in for a hug. "I didn't mean to upset you."

He leaned his head against my neck and let out a shaky breath. "Dunno why I'm upset. Tired, I guess."

"You're allowed to feel whatever you feel. Why don't you go lie down? I'll clean this up."

He looked at his plate like he hadn't noticed it before, then shook his head like the fog was back. "I'm sorry I'm kinda useless tonight."

"You're not useless, baby."

He pouted. "I wanted to make out some more tonight."

I chuckled. "I'm sure we can arrange something."

He gave me a lazy smile, but he got up from the table and limped to the couch. I cleaned up and he was asleep when I joined him. I commandeered the remote control and surfed through the channels for a few moments before his sleeping mind registered my presence. He curled into me, his head on my chest, and my arm went around his shoulder. I kissed the top of his head.

I hated that his mother's rejection had been playing on his mind. It brought out my protective side, which wasn't too pretty. But I'd be damned if I'd let that hateful bitch hurt him all over again. What she'd said to him, and how she'd said it, the last time he'd seen her had devastated him.

For all the memories he'd lost, I was glad he couldn't remember that.

And now, after all he'd been through, watching him deal with crippling pain, I couldn't bear the thought of anyone hurting him again. Instinctively, I tightened my hold and rubbed his arm, causing him to stir.

He lifted his head, his eyes half-closed, and he began to kiss me, clumsy and sleepy, but he shifted and climbed up to lie on top of me. He kissed me deep and I let him lead, setting whatever pace he needed.

It was slow and lovely, no pressure for anything else. Just kissing, tasting, and touching. He put his hands to my face, caressing and mapping out my features with his thumbs, as though he was committing every angle to memory.

He drew the kiss to a close and nuzzled into my neck. I half expected him to kiss me there, but he inhaled deeply and began to snore. And Squish chose that very moment to plant himself between us and the arm of the couch, and all I could do was laugh.

JUST ON SMOKO-TIME the next day, an old car pulled into the drive and Mr and Mrs Litchfield got out. Mrs Litchfield was holding a Tupperware container and Jimmy nervously flattened his shirt before they walked into the workshop.

I took a few long strides to meet them at the roller door opening and held out my hand. "Morning."

Jimmy shook my hand. "And what a good one it is," he said. "Thanks for agreeing to see me. I wasn't sure if it'd be too soon."

"Not at all," I replied. Then I turned around and called out, "Jusso? You got some visitors."

The workshop was kinda dark compared to the bright sunlight of outside, so it wasn't real easy to see. But Justin appeared on his scooter, wiping his hands on an oily rag. He was curious and trying to see their faces in the bright light. "Oh, hello," he said when he figured out who it was. "Hang on, let me lose the wheels."

He got up off his scooter and walked the last few steps to stand beside me. He shoved the rag into his back pocket and held out his hand, nodding to his arm. "I can shake your hand this time."

Jimmy shook his hand gently, smiled, and gave a nod. "Jimmy, and my wife, Nancy," he said. "You've come a long way since I last saw you. Up on your feet now."

"Yeah, mostly," Juss answered. "Still use the wheels to get around sometimes, especially down here in the workshop. It's much easier on my leg. Faster too."

Jimmy nodded again and wrung his hands. The poor guy was so nervous. "How about we go sit in the breakroom," I suggested.

"I made some biscuits," Nancy said. "Jam drops. Fresh this morning."

"Then a cup of tea sounds great," I added. "Come on through."

They sat at the old table in the breakroom while I made four cups of tea. Davo and Sparra came in and grabbed a cuppa and Nancy was quick to stand and offer them a biscuit. Davo was about to decline, but when Sparra grabbed two, saying his mum used to make jam drops like this, she just about beamed and Davo gave a polite nod and took a jam drop. It clearly made her happy, and Jimmy gave her a fond look. "We've been wondering how you've been getting on," he said.

"I'm getting better every day," Juss said. "I've got physio exercises and stuff that helps, but honestly, getting back to work has helped the most."

I smiled at that. "It has made a huge difference."

"I remember how to do everything," he furthered. "I can't remember much from the last five years, but I can still pull a two-stroke engine apart, clean it up, and put it back together in no time."

Jimmy smiled at that. "It must be a comfort."

Justin nodded. "It is."

Jimmy sipped his tea. "But your memory didn't come back?"

Juss gave a shake of his head. "Nah. Some things, but not much. I remembered Dallas, though. Just snippets of us." He smiled at me. "So it's not all bad news."

Jimmy got a little misty-eyed. "I'm glad to hear that." He cleared his throat. "I gotta say, I've been better since seein' you at the hospital. And I'm real grateful you don't mind us calling in today. It helps," he said, turning his cup of tea. "To know you're getting better."

"It helps me too," Justin said. "I told Dallas after you came to see me in the hospital that it helped putting a face to the accident." Jimmy's eyes widened, and Justin was quick to clarify. "Not in a bad way. In a good way. It wasn't some scary, unknown thing anymore. I can't remember the accident at all, and there was so much unknown always hanging over me. But now I know it was just that. It was an accident. And the guy driving the truck wasn't some bad guy who didn't give a shit. He was a nice guy who never meant to hurt me. And I dunno why, but that really helped."

Jimmy was teary now, and he nodded. "I get it, son. I know exactly what you mean." He smiled at his wife. "It helped me knowing you were both nice young fellas too. You showed me a kindness when you didn't have to."

Nancy nodded. "It means a lot to both of us." She

pulled her handbag onto her lap and pulled out a folded piece of cardboard. She handed it to Justin. "I hope you don't mind, but my granddaughter drew this for you. We babysit her some days when her mum works, and she knew that her poppy was sad about the accident and she wanted to help."

He opened the card, as it turned out, to see a crayon drawing. There was one couple, a man and a woman at the top of the page, and a second couple, two men, down at the bottom. There was a truck in between the two couples. The man at the top had a very big frown, and one of the men at the bottom had a broken leg and a broken arm, if the yellow squiggles were what I thought they were. It was very clearly done by a little kid.

There were also love hearts and shining sun and clouds in the top corner, and . . . "Is that a fish?" I asked.

"She just got a goldfish. She wanted to include it." Nancy nodded, giving me a sad smile. "She just turned five and she wanted to do something to help."

"It's amazing," Justin said. "What's her name?"

"Bethany."

"Please tell Bethany I said thank you. And it did make me feel better."

Jimmy was teary again. "She drew me one too. It's no secret that I haven't coped too well since the accident. I've told all my family what happened and how you two boys were so nice to me."

My God, these two were just the sweetest. "How many kids do you have?" I asked.

"Five children and twelve grandchildren," Nancy said. "Each one's a blessing."

To my surprise, though maybe it shouldn't have been,

Justin got a little teary. "You're real lucky to have such a big, happy family."

"You don't?" she asked him.

"I've got Dallas," he said with a smile in my direction. "And I have a sister and two nieces, who are just the cutest. They live in Sydney. My mother doesn't like my—" He made a face. "—choices."

Nancy reached over and took his hand. "It was never a choice for you, sweetheart."

I almost snorted my tea out my nose. "Oh, we know that. But thank you."

"Don't mind Nancy," Jimmy said fondly. "We've got a gay granddaughter, and my Nance protects her brood. Like a mother hen, she is. We don't care what walk of life the kids are, as long as they have manners and eat all their dinner." He gave a hard nod. "Oh, and I don't mind too much if they bring their old Pops some Turkish Delight every once in a while."

Justin and I both chuckled again, and Jimmy told us a story of being on the road a lot when his own kids were little and how he was real sorry about that, and how he was trying to make up for that with his grandkids. Then he asked Justin all about his recovery and how he was coping with it all. He and Nancy were such a genuine couple, we could have stayed chatting the whole day. I'd completely lost track of time when Davo knocked on the door.

He held out the office cordless phone. "Sorry, boss. But it's a call you need to take."

I frowned because I hadn't even heard the phone, and it wasn't like Davo not to either take the booking or take a message. I stood up. "Won't be long," I said, making my excuses as I left the room.

Davo handed me the phone. "Compo lady," he whispered.

"Oh shit, thank you." I clapped him on the arm as I went into my office and closed the door. My heart was in my throat, so much depended on this. "Dallas Muller speaking."

"Hi, Dallas, it's Angela Jarrett. Sorry I didn't get back to you sooner." I listened as she went through all the red tape and jargon I couldn't really follow. "Anyway, it's good news," she said. "It's been determined there was no vicarious liability by you or your employee."

Vicarious liability?

"What does that mean?"

"That you weren't at fault."

"Yeah, I'm aware of that."

"The van your employee was driving was in good working order, all safety precautions were made. Any and all modifications made to the storage area of the van were legal and did not contribute to the personal injury of your employee."

I was also aware of that. "So what does that mean? What do we do now?"

"The findings are in your favour. First of all, you'll be fully compensated for the van and the loss of income pertaining to the van and all the tools. I don't have a date for the recompense as yet."

I sagged with relief. It took me a second before I could speak. "And what about Justin?"

She paused. "I can't discuss his personal claim—"

"Yeah, but as his employer, what does this mean?"

"His wage compensation payment, or his personal injury benefit payments, will be ninety-five per cent of his income for thirteen weeks, then eighty-five per cent for the following fourteen weeks after that. You'll receive all backpay in full. He'll be reassessed after six months, which is standard." She paused. "I can tell you all his medical costs will be covered."

God, I could have cried. I actually had to try to swallow a few times before I could manage actual words. I squeezed my eyes closed and shook off my tears. "That's good news."

"It is. I'll be in touch when I have some dates of payment for you, but I'll send through an email confirming everything I have so far today and snail mail as well."

"Thank you. For everything."

She said goodbye and clicked off the call, and I just had to sit at my desk for a bit. I hadn't realised the weight I'd carried on my shoulders until it was gone. I felt so relieved, so fucking relieved, I couldn't even describe it.

All that worry, all that stress about money was over. I let out an almighty sigh just as I saw Justin by the door. Oh shit. I'd forgotten Jimmy and Nancy were here!

I met them all at the door just as they were leaving. "Sorry about that," I said.

"Oh, don't worry. I know you're busy," Jimmy said.

I didn't know what they'd talked about in my absence, but the three of them looked happy, though I could tell Juss was tired. We walked them out and waved them off, and Jimmy told us not to be strangers as he got into the car.

"Everything okay with that phone call?" Juss asked me.

"Couldn't have been better. It was the workers' compensation case manager. It's all been approved, for the van and your wages and all the medical bills."

Justin shot me a look. "For real? All of it?"

"For real, baby." I grinned at him. "Such a relief, right?"

He nodded. "You were really worried about it, weren't you?"

"Yeah. I was. But it's over now." I pulled him in for a hug just as Jimmy and Nancy drove out of the yard. They waved and we waved back, with Justin still pressed into my side. "Sorry for leaving you alone with them," I said.

"Oh no. It's fine. I really like them."

"Me too. They're a nice old couple."

"I'm glad. Because they invited us around for a barbeque next weekend. I said we'd go."

CHAPTER ELEVEN

I WAS SURPRISED, to say the least, that Juss agreed to a barbeque at Jimmy and Nancy's place. Having them call around to see how Justin was getting on was one thing, but going to their place was something else.

But this was something Justin decided he needed to do. It made him happy. And, the most important part, this was him making a decision and wanting to see it through. And being sociable and getting out of the house.

So who was I to disagree with that?

After Jimmy and Nancy left, Justin went upstairs and crashed out for a few hours and I read over the compensation claim information Angela had sent me. The van could be replaced, along with the thousands of dollars' worth of tools that had been in it. Ninety-five per cent of Juss' wage was covered, and one hundred per cent of the medical bills.

Yes, the relief I felt was immense but so was the gratitude. And with that in mind, after doing a little maths, I called Davo and Sparra into my office.

"What's up, boss?" Sparra asked.

"Take a seat, guys."

They both shot each other a nervous look as they sat.

"It's not bad," I said, easing their worries. "It's the opposite, actually. Justin's accident hit us pretty hard in a lot of ways and I'd be a shit boss if I didn't use that as an opportunity to implement a few things that would make your jobs easier and safer. So, I want you guys to have a think and put forward some ideas."

Davo cast me a cautious look. "Like what?"

"Well, I'm certain we could go through our toolkits and upgrade a few pieces, sure. Like new pressure kits and battery testers. That'll make all our jobs easier. But I was also thinking we could use some hydraulic hoists. I know we've been using old-school bike stands for years, but we should upgrade. They're safer and better for our backs. And that'll mean new shop seats as well."

"The fancy ones?" Sparra asked. "We can have scooter races with Jusso from one end of the workshop to the other."

I chuckled at that, and even Davo smiled. But then he shook his head. "Dallas," he whispered, "you don't need to do that."

"Yes I do. I should have done it years ago."

"Those hoists cost a fortune."

"We got the approval for workers' comp and insurance," I said. "Finally. And I should use the money to make everyone's job safer."

"Are we getting a new van?" Sparra asked.

"It's been approved, yeah." I let out a sigh. "But I'll be honest with ya's, I dunno how I feel about having someone on the road again. I know it was Justin's idea, it was his baby, and it was a good business decision, but the thought of another accident . . ." I shuddered. "I don't know if it's worth it."

"You'd worry about whoever went out now," Davo said quietly. And that was very true. I really would.

"Maybe Jusso will want to get back out there. Like you said, it was his idea to begin with. It was his job." Sparra shrugged. "Not sayin' I want him back out there either. I'm just saying it should be his choice. When he's right to drive again." His eyes met mine. "Will he ever be right to drive again?"

"Not for a while," I answered. "He'd have medical tests to get through and his neuro doctors would have to sign off on it. I think. We haven't really got that far yet. Definitely not for six months, I'd reckon."

Davo frowned. "But will he ever *want* to drive again? That's probably a better question. He can't remember the accident, but on some level, he'd have to be scared to get back behind the wheel, yeah? I know I would be."

That was a really good point. "He's been okay when we've been in the ute before," I said. "I think I was more worried about hearing some screeching tyres or something that might trigger something for him, but he seemed oblivious to it. Like getting into cars was no big deal at all. But you're right, Davo. Whether he'll ever be up for driving again is a really good question."

***

"HEY," I said, walking into the flat. Justin hadn't come back downstairs, so I was surprised to see him lying on the couch with a blanket and Squish. The TV was on but the volume was on real low, not that he was watching it anyway. "Everything okay?"

"Yeah," he said. "Just got a bit of a headache, that's all. Thought I'd take it easy."

I sat beside him and put the back of my hand to his forehead. He wasn't running a temp, thank God. "Sure you're okay?"

He gave a tired smile. "I put a frozen lasagne in the oven, but I didn't know what you'd want to have with it. I'm not real hungry."

I lifted his chin, ever so slightly, and looked into his eyes. "On a scale of one to ten, how bad is your headache?"

He slow blinked and tried to smile. "'Bout a six."

"A six? Your six would be my nine, Juss, because you know what an actual nine or ten feels like," I whispered. "Baby, you should have messaged me. I would've come up."

"I'm okay. Just taking it easy."

"Did you take your pills?"

He nodded and took my hand, threading our fingers. "Yeah. At three."

Shit. And his pain was still a six. In hindsight, I should have checked on him when he didn't come back down. "I got busy and lost track of time. I should have come up. I'm sorry."

"'S okay, Dall. It's not too bad. I just didn't want to overdo it, that's all."

Which was a good thing, I allowed. And a good sign that he recognised the need to rest. "Can I get you anything? A juice or a cup of tea?"

He smiled. "A cuddle. Always makes me feel better."

"I can do that."

"A proper lie-down cuddle," he added. "And you can rub circles on my back and put your fingers through my hair."

Chuckling, I shuffled down a bit and lay beside him on my side, boots still on and all. But he quickly pressed himself into my chest, one arm under his head, the other drawing lazy patterns on his back. "That better?" I whispered.

"So much better."

We lay like that for a few minutes and I stroked his back and his head like he asked. His face became peaceful, his breathing even. I could watch him sleep forever. I hated that he lived with such awful headaches, though.

And I could finally lie with him without the dark cloud of money hanging over me. I didn't realise just how much it had overshadowed me. Like I could breathe deep and exhale properly for the first time in weeks.

The oven timer went off and I groaned. "Oh man, I'm sorry," I whispered, extracting my arm from under his head. I planted a kiss on the scar above his ear and went to rescue the lasagne. I served up mine with some salad and cut Juss a small piece of the lasagne as well. He said he didn't want to eat, but maybe he could have a few bites, especially if he'd had pain meds.

He begrudgingly sat up and held Squish away from the food, and I fed Juss small bites of dinner in between forkfuls of my own. When I was done and satisfied he'd eaten enough, we lay back down on the couch with Juss as the little spoon, and he fought sleep long enough to take his meds, then go to bed.

I tidied up and watched the rest of the Friday night footy, but the movie after that was crap so I showered and went to bed. Justin was sound asleep—his pain meds would knock him out pretty hard—but as soon as I was in the bed beside him, he stirred and somehow sensed that I was close and snuggled right into me and went straight back to a deep sleep.

All he'd ever wanted was to feel loved. To be held, to be protected and safe; everything that had been lacking in his life, everything his mother never gave him. So, even though he was out like a light, I held him a little tighter. "I love you, Justin Keith." I planted a soft kiss to his forehead and closed my eyes. "Always have, always will."

A SEX DREAM woke me up. An amazing dream where I was on top of Justin, inside him. He was rocking his hips and I drove into him with his upswing. God, it was so good, I didn't want it to ever end. But it flitted away like dreams sometimes do and it took a second for reality to kick in.

A reality of being on our sides, pressed up against Justin's back, and . . . oh, sweet mother of God, he was rocking his hips.

"Morning," he rasped. "Didn't think you'd ever wake up."

"Fuck, sorry," I said, trying to get my mind in gear.

He put a hand on my hip. "Don't move."

Of course, I froze and it gave me a split second to take stock of my body and where exactly my dick was for it to feel that good. My erection was pressed between his legs, between his arse cheeks, behind his balls . . . Oh God.

"Feels good," he murmured.

"Oh fuck." My hips curled without my permission, seeking more . . . of everything that felt so good.

I kissed the back of his neck, his shoulder, and tried to get my hips under control. I wanted to thrust so bad. But then, just like in my dream, he rolled his hips, pulling on my cock. It hadn't been a dream. It was Justin getting off on my cock.

Was that his arm moving? Was he jerking off?

Oh, fucking hell, he was.

"Fuck, you feel so good," I ground out.

"God, Dallas." He flexed his hips, rolling and rocking on my erection between his legs.

It was almost too much to bear. "I'll come if you keep doing that."

He groaned and did it harder.

Fuck.

I began to thrust gently in time with his tempo, and after only a few more thrusts, I gripped his hip and he cried out. At first I thought I'd hurt him, but he went rigid against me and convulsed as he came.

His arse cheeks clenched around my shaft and I followed his lead, spilling hot come between his legs, behind his balls.

"Oh God, Justin," I growled, and he arched back, relaxing into my arms. He was spent and breathing hard.

We were both rattled with aftershocks, and I held him tight. I didn't pull back. I wanted to be as close to him as I possibly could. "That was crazy," he said with a gravelly laugh. "I woke up like that. You were hard and sliding your cock against me for a while. It felt so good, so thank you."

"I was dreaming," I replied, chuckling. I kissed his shoulder again. "I was having this hot sex dream and I woke up to find out it wasn't a dream at all."

"Well, the bed's a mess. I'm a mess." He wiggled his arse a little and I pulled my sensitive dick away. "We need to shower and change the sheets."

I was reluctant to let go of him. "How's your head feeling?"

"'S okay. It'll be better when you wash me in the shower, then feed me breakfast."

I laughed. He was obviously feeling better, and he

wasn't even his usual morning-grumpy self. I kissed the back of his head. "Your wish, my command."

WORK WAS steady for the next few days and Justin's headaches subsided enough for him to work again. He really was happier when he was busy, getting his hands dirty and being productive.

There really wasn't that much difference between the old Justin and the new Justin. He was never happier than when he was working on a bike. He was still on light duties and always worked paired with someone, and he still needed a rest around lunchtime. Though he was coming back downstairs mid-afternoon to resume his work.

The improvements every day were small, but in hindsight, I could see him come so far.

He was happier, and I was certainly a lot less stressed now I knew the insurance and compensation money were all approved. It wasn't in the bank yet, and I was still swapping money around to pay for stuff, but knowing it was coming was a helluva relief. Davo and Sparra were happier too; morale was high because I included them in deciding which work improvements we should prioritise. I really did value all they did for me and their opinions, but I wanted to give them something else as a token of my appreciation.

So, given it was Friday and I had to go to the bank, I told them all I'd bring back an early lunch. At the bank, I had them increase my business credit card limit an extra ten grand. Not something I'd ever wanted to do, but now I knew the insurance and compo money were coming, it would take the pressure off.

Afterward, I swung past Charlestown Square shopping

centre and picked up a whole stack of Japanese dumplings plus a surprise something for the breakroom.

When I got back to the workshop, I carried the bag with my surprise in it through to the breakroom along with the takeout containers. "Lunch is here."

Tools down, the three of them followed me in. I opened the dumplings and grabbed some forks and pointed to each container. "Beef, chicken, pork."

"Whatcha got there?" Juss asked, nodding to the big bag behind me.

"A little surprise and a thank you," I said. I lifted the box out of the bag and set it on the counter. "I thought it was about time we did away with the instant coffee and got some real stuff."

It was just one of those pod machines that everyone had these days and something I'd heard the boys talking about. I pulled out a few packets of the pods to go with it, even some decaf ones for Juss.

"Oh, hell yes," Sparra crowed, his mouth half full of dumpling. "We're drinking the fancy shit now."

"And that's not all," I said, suddenly nervous. I pulled two envelopes out of my back pocket and handed one to Davo and one to Sparra. "From me to you both. As thanks, for everything."

Davo opened his and took out the piece of paper. It was a bank cheque for a thousand bucks. His eyes shot to mine. "Dallas . . ."

Sparra opened his with less finesse and pulled out the cheque. "What is it?" He read it and shot a confused glance to Davo, then me. "Is that for me?"

"Money was tight for a while, not gonna lie. But now the insurance has all been approved, I can breathe again. I wanted to thank you both. For everything you guys did while Juss and me couldn't be here. You really stepped up and got us through a really hard time."

"What is it?" Juss asked. Sparra showed him the cheque and Juss looked at me with a soft smile. "You did that for them?"

I nodded. "I was gonna book the four of us in for the MotoGP on Phillip Island, or maybe the motocross championship finals on the Sunshine Coast. I couldn't decide, but then I thought the cash might be better. Sparra, I know you've been eyeing off a new pair of riding boots and a set of Pirelli's. And Davo, I know you and Lauren wanted to fix up the back patio at your place." I shrugged. "Or whatever you want to spend it on, I dunno. It's your money."

"I wouldn't have said no to a trip to the Grand Prix," Davo said with a smile. "But this is . . . I didn't expect this. Not sure what to say, actually."

"Same," Sparra said. "Thanks, Dallas. And Jusso. You paid us for all the overtime. We didn't expect nothing extra."

"I know," I replied. "I wanted to do it."

"And a coffee machine!" Davo said. "You weren't messing around."

I rolled my eyes. "Yeah, and you guys are gonna have to show me how to use it."

Juss pulled out the seat next to him at the table and patted it. I sat, and we ate all the dumplings and talked and laughed. It felt so good to give them something back. Not that the money was an amount of their worth, but just a small thanks to let them know what they did to help me out didn't go unnoticed.

As we talked and ate, Juss kept his hand on my thigh, and when Davo and Sparra decided to get the coffee machine up and running, Juss leaned over and kissed the tip of my shoulder. "You're a really good guy, you know that?" he whispered.

"I wanted to say thanks, that's all."

Juss looked at me with such love. "I'm pretty sure that's another reason why I overlooked the fact you're a Bulldogs supporter," he said with a wink.

I laughed, and Davo and Sparra argued about the coffee machine and whether it needed a cycle of water through it first, and Sparra was adding water to it while Davo was reading the instruction booklet. They bickered like old hens, and Juss laughed as he slipped his hand in mine. He put his tired head on my shoulder and I could feel him vibrate every time he chuckled.

A few minutes and a full comedy routine later, we had our first taste of coffee, and I had to admit, it was so much better. Davo and Sparra both thanked me for lunch and went back to their workstations, and Juss sat up and stretched his back.

"You okay?" I asked.

"Yeah. Just tired. I might head upstairs for a bit."

"Okay. I'll help you."

"Nah, it's okay. I can manage."

"I was really just using that as an excuse to check your arse out on the way up the stairs, and maybe steal a proper kiss when we get inside."

He laughed. "Well, that's okay then. I'll allow that."

We walked out of the breakroom just as Sparra was reaching for the old stereo. "Hell yes. Some classic Chisel!" he crowed just before he turned the volume up.

"When the War Is Over" was playing. God, I loved this song. Juss and I had danced to this song when we first got together. I turned to Justin, smiling, wondering if he might remember this song as ours, only to see him stop.

Frozen.

His face blank but somehow horrified.

Then his right eye closed, then his left. Both squinted shut and he put his hand to the right side of his head, to his scar, and he swayed.

And then he screamed.

CHAPTER TWELVE

"JUSTIN!" I grabbed hold of his arm. "Justin, are you okay?"

His right eye squinted shut and he fell into me. "I remember . . ."

Holding Justin, I glanced at Davo. "Call an ambulance."

"No, no ambulance. No hospital," Justin said, putting his hand out. "I'm okay. My head . . . God, I remember."

Sparra appeared with a chair from the breakroom and I lowered Justin into it. I knelt in front of him. He was pale and sweating, and his right eye being closed was scaring the shit out of me. It hadn't been like that for weeks. "Juss, you don't look too good."

He put his hand to his head; his right eye was still squinted closed. "I don't feel too good."

Davo upended an old ice cream container, spilling old bolts and washers onto the floor. He handed it to me and I put it on Juss' lap. "How bad is the pain? From one to ten."

He shook his head. "Dallas, I remember. Driving the van. This song. 'When the War Is Over.' It came on the radio. It's our song, Dall. I remember. The light was green. It was just getting to Jimmy Barnes' part of the song."

He was panting and still so pale. But his eye. His eye squinting like that scared me the most.

"I can hear the brakes and horns. And it's pissing rain. I turned to see out my window, Dallas, and the truck is right there. The grille is right there."

He put his hand up to his right, as though he could touch the truck in his memory.

"Then there was glass and metal. My head. God, the pain, I can feel the pain. It's bad. Then the darkness." He sobbed. "That awful nothingness in my dreams. That's all that's left. Just darkness and pain."

"Oh, Juss," I whispered, my hands to his face.

He began to cry and curl in on himself. "Oh my God, I remember it. Our song was playing, and the truck didn't stop. It hurts so bad, Dall. I can feel how much it hurt."

His right eye didn't seem to want to open at all, and I worried that he was having some kind of stroke. "Juss, I need you to look at me. Can you open your mouth for me? Show me your teeth?"

Tears spilled down his cheeks. "What the fuck for?"

Stunned for a second, I laughed with relief. His brain and mouth were working just fine. "I was just worried about . . . your right eye's closed. I was just checking for a stroke."

He was still far too pale and sweating, but his breathing was better at least. He put his hand to his head. "Christ, my head just hurts. Like when I first woke up in hospital. Like the truck just hit me, all over again."

"Is the pain too much, Juss?" I asked, looking up at him. "I can call an ambulance—"

"No." He squinted and put the heel of his hand against

his scar. "Just need pills and sleep. No hospital. I don't want to go back to hospital, Dall. Please. Please. I can't go back."

"Okay, okay," I said, trying to calm him. The last thing he needed right now, was to be more upset. "We'll get you to bed. But Juss, if it gets worse, you have to tell me."

He nodded, but I could tell the exhaustion was kicking in.

"I'm gonna pick you up and carry you upstairs, okay?"

He nodded again, and the fact he didn't even want to try to do it on his own told me all I needed to know. I carried him up the stairs and put him straight on the bed. I pulled off his boots, got his pills, which he also took without argument.

"That song, Dall," he whispered. "'S our song."

My heart hurt, good and bad. "Yeah, baby. It's our song." I kissed his forehead. "Go to sleep."

"When the War Is Over." Appropriate for a whole other lot of reasons now. When would this war be over? Would it ever end for him?

I was beginning to think it wouldn't.

I watched his beautiful face as he slept, his parted lips, his closed eyelids, and took out my phone.

***

"I GAVE him his heavy-duty pills. He's sleeping."

"Okay, that's good," Doctor Chang said. I'd called her office and told her what had happened. The whole flashback had freaked me out just as much as it had Justin. "Memory flashbacks can trigger the memory of physical pain," she said. Then she spoke for a bit on psychosomatic something or other and it was comforting to hear her say what Justin experienced was okay. It wasn't uncommon or unusual, and what I did was right, and having him resting right now was the best thing for him.

Having that reassurance was a godsend. "Thank you."

"You have an appointment on Tuesday, so I'll see you both then," she said. "But if his headaches get any worse, or if he experiences more dizziness or nausea, fever or anything like that, take him to outpatients and call me."

"I will. Thank you."

I clicked off the call and sat on the edge of the bed. He was out like a light, so I went back downstairs to let Davo and Sparra know he was okay. Davo was working on a bike and Sparra was cleaning down his station. They both stopped what they were doing and came over, and I noticed the radio was off.

"How is he?" Sparra asked.

"He's okay. He's sleeping right now. I spoke to the doc. She said it wasn't unheard of to experience the pain associated with a memory, especially in amnesia patients." I shrugged. "Which is good. If she was concerned, I'd have him back at the ER."

Davo clapped my arm. "He'll be all right."

"Kinda scary, though," Sparra added. "That a song could trigger a memory. I didn't know, otherwise I wouldn't have turned it up."

"You weren't to know. None of us were. Hell, not even Justin knew until he heard it. Some memory wire in his brain tripped, and it was like the truck hitting him all over again."

Davo studied me for a bit. "I would suggest taking you out tonight and getting shitfaced, but I know you won't leave him."

I smiled at that. "Maybe next weekend the four of us can go out and grab a pub feed and watch the footy. We won't be drinking, though, but getting out might be a good idea."

"Deal." Davo looked back to his workstation. "We can finish up here if you wanna go back upstairs."

I scrubbed my hand over my face. "How about the three of us hook in and get everything done so we can all clock out early?"

"Done!" Sparra said quickly, and that's what we did. Davo finished up on the bike he was working on, and by the time the customer came to collect it, me and Sparra had the whole place cleaned and ready to be locked up.

I pulled the roller door shut and both the guys thanked me for lunch, the coffee machine, and their bonus cheques. It felt like that all happened a week ago.

"See ya's Monday, bright and early," I said.

"Call us if you need anything over the weekend," Sparra said, and Davo nodded.

God, I loved these blokes. "Will do."

I locked the gate behind them and raced up the stairs. Justin was still sound asleep, now with Squish keeping guard, so I left them to it and made a start on dinner. I was torn between wanting home-cooked comfort food and not being arsed to do anything but call for a pizza, but it was cold outside and I wanted comfort. I threw a bunch of stuff into a casserole dish to make up some kind of goulash stew and set it in the oven, had a steaming hot shower, and changed into some trackies, socks, and a hoodie.

I poked my head into the bedroom and found Justin awake. He was lying on his side, stroking Squish. "Hey," I whispered.

He smiled. "Hey."

"How're you feeling?"

"Okay. The drugs work."

I chuckled and sat beside him. Both of his eyes were open, though heavy-lidded. "I'm glad."

"I woke up and you weren't here, but I could hear you so it was okay."

I rubbed his hip. "I'm never far away, baby."

"I know." He closed his eyes for a bit. "Sorry about before. In the shop."

"Don't apologise. You have nothing to be sorry about."

"It just hit me," he said. "The memory. The song. The pain." *The truck . . .*

"It must have been scary as hell."

"Yeah."

"I spoke to Doctor Chang. I called her to ask if we should come to the hospital and she said no, just to keep an eye on you. She said what you experienced wasn't uncommon. But if you get dizzy or more headaches, she wants to see us."

He gave a bit of a nod, and his right eye was back to normal: a sign the worst of the pain was gone. "I hate it, ya know," he murmured. "I hate that you have to look after me, that I have these problems. I feel like an invalid."

"Hey." I took his hand and waited for him to make eye contact. "Juss, I love looking after you. It's not a problem. It's just what we need to do right now. It won't always be this way. And even if it was, I'd still do it. Together forever, remember?"

He smiled. "No, I don't. Amnesia, remember?"

I chuckled and leaned down for a kiss. "Dinner's in the oven. I made some kind of pasta stew. I thought we could bring the doona out to the couch and have a bowl of comfort food and watch the footy. Just take it real easy."

He sat up slowly and gave me a nudge. "You don't have

to do that for me. I know I'm kinda fuzzy on those painkillers, but I feel okay."

I sighed, my heart suddenly heavy. "I know, Juss. But I think tonight I need to do it for me."

His gaze shot to mine. "Oh."

"I'm just feeling a bit raw this arvo," I admitted. "I dunno why. Just want a quiet night holed up under the doona with you, that's all." I tried not to cry but my eyes burned with tears and in the end, I just let them fall. I didn't want to hide this from him.

"Dall?"

"I'm okay," I said, wiping my cheek. "I'm just... I dunno. Relieved about the money, like a huge weight is off me. And I was worried about you this afternoon. I guess I reached a limit."

Juss frowned. "I'm sorry."

"You don't have to apologise," I replied, giving him a smile despite my tears. "But Juss, sometimes I'm not as strong as I need to be."

"I know I lean on you for everything. But you don't need to be strong all the time."

"I want you to lean on me, to need me. I like being that for you. I like being the protector and the provider. But I dunno, I've been so stressed and worried. I just feel a bit low right now and I need to be with you tonight. Just us and nothing else."

He nodded and squeezed my hand. "I'm sorry I didn't think of you. Anything you want, Dall."

"I want to block the world out and I want to know you're okay, that's all."

He leaned over and kissed the side of my head. "Then let's do that."

Juss picked up Squish and I pulled the doona and

pillows off the bed and we made ourselves a nest on the couch. It was raining outside now, and with only the light in the kitchen on, it felt cosy and warm inside our little cocoon. We ate bowls of stew and watched the Friday night footy with the volume down low, and for the first time in our relationship, I was the little spoon.

I lay with my back to Juss' front, and he either had his arm around me or his hand stroking my hair. It felt so damn nice to be taken care of, just this once. I'd always assumed the role of protector. Even as a teenager, I was always looking out for the kids who couldn't defend themselves. I was always taller and bigger—I was already six foot at fifteen years old—and sure, even the arsehole kids at my high school knew I was gay and they only tried to back me into a corner once. I put three of them on their arses and the fourth ran away.

I was always the protector, the defender, the one who would wrap my arms around them and tell them it was all gonna be okay. But tonight it was me who needed it, and I couldn't even say why.

Maybe it was a combined meltdown of the last month, all the stress and worry, the relief of the workers' comp being approved, and then the uncertainty of Juss' episode today. But I just needed . . . reassurance.

After trying to hold it all together for so long, I felt like I was barely holding on.

"You okay?" Juss asked. He stroked my hair, then gently scratched my beard.

I shuffled onto my back, though there wasn't much room. "I am now," I murmured. "I feel better."

He had his head propped up on his arm as he studied my eyes and ran his thumb along my bottom lip before cupping my face. "I'm sorry I didn't think of what you need."

"Juss," I began.

"No, please, hear me out. Everything since my accident has been about me. Every minute of every day, and to be honest, I haven't been able to think of anyone else. I mean, I think of you, of course. But when I was still all foggy, I couldn't think of anything. Then it was just all about my recovery, my body, my brain. Managing pain and physio and trying to get my brain to think normally. And you . . ." He thumbed my cheek. "You were just always this *mountain* of strength, and throughout this whole thing, you never took a backward step. God, Dallas, even when I didn't remember you, you still showed up every day. You never gave up; you never doubted our love." He got a little teary. "And I never stopped to think that you might need . . . something. Anything."

"Juss, I just felt a bit down, that's all."

"But that's my point. You know all my moods, you know how I'm feeling, and I don't even have to say a word. You just know. And I want to be like that for you."

"But you are. I said I needed a night where we could block out the world and you did that for me."

He made a face as though he didn't really agree. "I just want you to know I'm going to try harder. I want to be for you what you are for me."

I touched the side of his face. "And what's that?"

"Everything. Dallas, you're everything to me."

That made my heart full and my tummy swoop. "And you're everything to me as well."

He tapped his finger to the tip of my nose. "And you giving Davo and Sparra that money today was really great," he whispered. "I don't think I realised how stressed you were about the money."

"I didn't want you to worry." I scanned his face. "But I was, yeah. And now we don't have to worry. I mean, I'm not gonna go crazy. I just wanted to show Davo and Sparra how much I appreciate them."

"Just proves what kind of guy you are. And how I'm so lucky to be with you."

I leaned up and kissed him. "I love you, Justin."

"And I love you, so much." He kissed me this time, allowing his body to fall onto mine. I let him set the pace he was comfortable with and there was more urgency this time. More passion, more desire, and he could no doubt feel my body react. I could certainly feel his. He pulled his lips from mine. "Do you think we could go to bed. This lounge isn't great for my leg and the drugs are wearing off and I really want to keep making out."

I chuckled. "Bed sounds great."

"I just can't decide if I want a shower before or after orgasms."

I burst out laughing and put my hand to his face. "Shower. Then you can go straight to sleep while you're all blissed out."

"You really do know me so well."

I peeled myself out from underneath him and carefully helped him to his feet. I let him get his equilibrium before helping him into the shower. "You know, I could do this by myself," he said.

"Oh, I know you could."

He smirked. "You just like to be thorough."

I chuckled. "And you like me being thorough."

"I really do."

He washed himself and I stayed right there in case the

steam and hot water made him dizzy, and I handed him a towel when he shut the water off. His erection was still half-hard, though his blinks were a little slow. He was getting tired. "We better get you to bed."

"Yes, you better." He looked at his PJs but didn't put them on. "I want to sleep naked with you. I want to be close to you all night."

"Sounds good to me." God, it sounded like heaven to me.

We got into bed and I stripped down to nothing and slid in beside him. He was all warm and he smelt clean and delicious. "I'm sleepy, Dallas," he murmured.

"I know, baby."

"So you better do the orgasms quick."

I snorted out a laugh. "Is that right?"

"Yeah. I know I'm supposed to take care of you tonight, but I can't do . . . I can't kneel or bend or do stuff like that."

That was all the permission I needed to get. I rolled on top of him and took our cocks into my hand. "I'll always take care of you, baby," I whispered, sliding our shafts together. "Just like this."

"Holy shit." Justin squinted his eyes shut.

I froze, thinking I'd hurt him. "You okay?"

"Don't stop. Please. Christ. Don't stop." He hooked his left leg up, his knee to my ribs. He opened his eyes as though his own leg had surprised him. "Dallas . . ."

"I know, baby," I whispered. Because I did know. I knew exactly what he meant, what he felt, what he couldn't put into words.

I knew, because I felt it too.

I slid our cocks in my fist, holding my weight off him the best I could. But I was between his legs, and with his left leg hitched up in this position, I could have so easily been inside him. He nodded like he thought the same, then his eyes rolled back and he drove his cock up and spilled his orgasm between us.

The sight of him, the smell of our desire, the feel of his pulsing cock, and I followed over the edge with him.

Justin put his hand to my neck and brought me down for a kiss and the full weight of my body on his, and we kissed until our passion simmered into sleepy nudges. Justin was almost asleep, but he kept his arms around me.

"I need to get us cleaned up," I murmured.

"Mmm." He dropped his arms to his side. "Hurry."

I unstuck our bellies, making him chuckle, though his eyes stayed closed. I cleaned us both up, and as soon as I was back in bed with him, he clung to me like he always did. "Love you, Juss," I whispered with a kiss to his forehead. "Always have."

He mumbled sleepily. "Always will."

CHAPTER THIRTEEN

DALLAS WASN'T sure we should attend the barbeque lunch at Jimmy and Nancy's place because of my little episode with the memory pain the day before, but I felt good.

In some way, I felt better because I could remember it.

It was scary and the pain that hit me along with the flashback was nauseatingly real. But I could remember it. I could remember how and why my whole life changed, and that was, in some fucked-up way, reassuring.

But now, I could see the memory in my mind and there was no pain with it anymore.

I woke up pressed against Dallas and his enormous dick was squashed against my arse cheek. It felt so good, that familiar buzz in my belly, that drawing-down feeling in my balls.

My body was starting to like the idea of doing more with Dallas, and my mind was too. I knew it would happen; it was only a matter of time. The night before, when he was between my legs and holding my cock against his, it was so much like making love, and for a fleeting second, I'd wanted it.

Not quite yet.

But soon.

"Juss, you okay? You zoned out there for a minute."

"Yeah, sorry. Was just thinking . . ."

"About?"

"I dunno, stuff."

"Pleasant stuff, I take it. Because you were smiling."

"Yeah, okay, I was thinking about you."

Dallas' whole face lit up when he smiled. "Really?"

"Yeah, of course." Man, to see him smile like that . . . "I think about you all the time."

"Good thoughts, I hope."

He looked at me in a way that made my heart feel too big for my chest. "Always. There's bits and pieces in my head that I don't know if are real memories or parts of dreams. I can't remember anything I dreamed of in the last five years either. But I see snippets that I think are real."

"Such as?"

"You yelling on the phone to a dodgy supplier for fucking up an order. You laughing at something Sparra said. You walking out of the bathroom naked. You making me coffee in the morning." I shrugged. "But it's not really what I see. It's what I feel. When you put your arm around me, or if you take my hand while we were watching TV. I just feel so happy, right here." I tapped my breastbone. "And I dunno if I'm remembering something that happened or something I dreamed, because I'm pretty sure I'd feel the same. Real hand-holding or dream hand-holding, it'd all feel the same to me."

"You'd be happy if you dreamed that I held your hand?"

"Sure I would."

"Does it feel real?"

"Yeah. And the clothes you're wearing seem real. Like actual T-shirts we own, and I'm sure if it were all in my dreams, you wouldn't be wearing any clothes."

He laughed at that but then met my eyes. "Sounds like you're remembering a lot more than you realise."

"Yeah, maybe. Nothing concrete. Nothing like yesterday when I remembered the accident."

"Did you want to talk about it?"

I shrugged again. "Not really. There's not much to say. I was going to a job at Glendale, it was pissing down rain, and our song came on the radio."

"I never realised it was *our* song," he said.

"It's our song, unofficially. I guess. I remember thinking as I was singing along that we didn't really have a song, but if we did, that would be it. But I can't remember why I thought it was our song."

He smiled thoughtfully. "We danced to it at the Lion's Arms pub. We'd been together about a month."

"We danced at the Lion's Arms? Together?" That pub wasn't exactly gay-central.

"We did. We were drunk."

"Obviously."

He laughed. "You were drinking Bundy."

I made a face. "God, I hate that stuff. I haven't drunk that in . . . well, I don't know how long it's been. Literally, I have no clue."

He chuckled again with kindness in his eyes. "You haven't touched it again since that night. But yeah, we danced to that song. And if I can remember correctly, we sang along pretty badly."

It was those things I missed the most. The memories of the little moments, things that seem insignificant or silly but the parts that make everything so real. "I wish I could remember that."

He lifted my hand to his lips and kissed my palm. "I know you do, baby." Still holding my hand, he met my eyes. "Are you sure you still want to go?"

I nodded. "I said we would, and I'd like to." Then it occurred to me that maybe he didn't want to go to Jimmy and Nancy's place for a barbeque lunch, and he had to take me because I had no other way to get there. "Dallas, if you don't want to come . . ."

"No, it's not that I don't want to, it's just that I worry you might overdo it. Or it might get too much. I dunno. We haven't really gone anywhere, apart from the supermarket and to the doctor's offices. Especially after yesterday. Remembering the accident . . ."

"Dall, I'm okay. I feel pretty good. And I know better than to overdo it. We won't stay long. I'll be falling asleep at their table if we stay too long."

"Okay, if you're sure."

"I'm sure."

And I really didn't know why I was so sure. But I wanted to go. I really liked old Jimmy and Nancy. They were sweet and kind, and I hadn't had a lot of that in my life. It felt rude to turn down their invitation, and if it became weird, Dallas and I would just leave.

But it wasn't weird . . . Well, not in a bad way. When we arrived, we weren't the only ones there. Jimmy and Nancy's house was an old but cute little white house with a small porch with flowerpots hanging from the beam, an old concrete path, and immaculate grass and gardens. As soon as we walked through the door, we were bombarded with the smell of good food and the sound of chatter and laughter.

"Come in, come in," Nancy said, ushering us down a short hall through a kitchen and family room to the back door. "Everyone's out the back. Go on through." Then she hollered at the door. "Jimmy? Look who's here."

The backyard was a fair size with tidy lawns and gardens, a small shed to the side, kids playing soccer, and a circle of a dozen people all sitting around on camping chairs. Jimmy put his drink on the table and welcomed us. "Boys, come on out and let me introduce you."

He went around the chairs with names I had no hope of remembering, but there were smiles and nods and warm welcomes. Jimmy and Nancy's kids were all older than us, and I realised some of the younger folk closer to our age sitting around were Jimmy's grandkids. "We're just neighbours," one guy said about himself and the woman sitting next to him.

"And we're just ring-ins," another guy said. "Grew up a few doors down and still come back for Nancy's caramel tart."

Everyone laughed and someone else mentioned some other food as their conversation broke away, and Jimmy looked up at me. "No wheels today?" he asked, motioning toward my leg.

"My scooter? It's in the ute," I replied. "Leg's feeling okay today. Not sure how long that'll last though."

"Here," Jimmy said, pulling up a seat. "Take a load off."

I sat and Dallas found a chair beside me, and Jimmy offered us a drink. "Oh, we can't drink," I explained. "Dallas is driving and I can't drink alcohol anymore."

Jimmy stopped. "I've been on the wagon for thirty years. All I got here is lemonade, ginger beer, or water." He picked up the can he'd put on the table. "I fancy a lemonade, but now Nancy's got me on that sugar-free stuff."

"So you don't get diabetes, Dad," one guy said.

Jimmy smiled and rolled his eyes. "Yeah, yeah."

We took our ginger beers and Nancy called out for Jimmy to check the meat, and when he went off to the barbeque, the guy sitting next to me turned out to be Jimmy's son. "Dad hoped you'd show up today," he said. "He told us he and Mum called around to see how you were getting on."

"Ah yeah." I wasn't sure what else to say. Clearly they knew all about us and all about the accident, no doubt. "I didn't know it was a family thing."

"Ah, no," he said, smiling just like his dad. "Mum and Dad have been having these lunches every month or two for as long as I can remember. Anyone who's anyone comes along. Old friends, current neighbours, and even the old neighbours who moved away but we can't get rid of." The caramel-tart guy raised his beer to that, making us smile.

Apparently Jimmy and Nancy had lived in this house for fifty years and Jimmy grew all kinds of veggies in the back gardens and they'd swap goods with other houses in the street. For a few zucchinis, capsicums, and tomatoes, they'd get fresh eggs from Beverly, dried salamis from old Cranky Franky. "And Dad's new favourite neighbours, Ensar and Nida. Ensar makes the real Turkish Delight. The real, traditional stuff."

Jimmy turned around at the barbeque and whisper-shouted, "And don't you say anything about it to your mother."

A woman laughed. "She knows where your stash is, Dad."

I laughed at that, then someone else asked if Ensar and Nida were coming today, but no, their son had some soccer thing on. And so it went on. It was like something out of a family TV show, where everyone was nice and genuine and just really good people.

People played some musical chairs as they all chatted with everyone else, and a woman ended up sitting next to me. She introduced herself again. "Kathy, Mum and Dad's youngest." Apparently, it was her daughter Bethany who had drawn the picture with the fish. Kathy pointed out a little blonde girl with the other kids.

"You've got a great crew here," Dallas said, nodding toward where the kids were now playing a game of chase while the adults laughed.

"We weren't supposed to bring anything, were we?" I asked. "Your mum told me not to bring anything, but I feel bad."

Kathy shook her head. "Oh no. She does the lot. Always has. Spends all week cooking. If not for us, for the women's auxiliary or the Rotary Club. She'd be offended if you brought something. And Dad's in charge of the barbie. He just does what Mum tells him, basically." She winked.

"Oh, okay," I said with a laugh. "Yeah, your mum brought some biscuits around the other day when they called in. They were delicious."

Kathy's smile saddened a little. "Dad was devastated about the accident. He was so upset that someone got hurt."

I noticed that other chatter had died off. They were listening now, curious to hear about the crash, I guess. Jimmy had taken a tray of meat inside the house, so now was the best time to broach the subject. "Yeah, he came to see me at the hospital," I said.

Dallas put his hand on my arm and he smiled at Kathy. "Your dad was quite nervous that day, but he seemed genuine. I wasn't sure what to expect, but he was very nice."

Kathy gave a nod and smiled sadly at me. "He said you were in a bad way."

"Yeah. I got busted up pretty bad."

Everyone was watching me and listening now, and Jimmy came back out and took his seat. He gave me a nod to continue.

"I have two metal plates in my leg," I said, looking down at my right leg. "My arm was broken here and here." I pointed to my forearm and below my shoulder. "And I have this," I said, turning a little and lifting my hair so they could see the huge scar down my head. "How many staples was it, Dall?"

"In his leg and head, sixty-two staples and nineteen stitches," he answered, smiling at me. "A fractured skull, fractured orbital socket, and a subdural haematoma."

I nodded. "And I lost five years' worth of memories," I added. "Five years of my life were just gone."

Dallas took my hand. "When he woke up, he thought he was twenty-five and living in Darwin."

Kathy looked horrified. "You had no memory of Dallas?"

I shook my head. "Nope."

"That was the worst part for me," Jimmy said. "The hardest part. I couldn't imagine waking up one day and not knowing who my Nance is."

The girl next to Jimmy patted his leg. "It's all right, Pop."

I hadn't meant for the mood to sour so much, but she had asked me about the accident. I wasn't going to lie about it.

"Do you remember anything now?" Kathy asked.

"Some things, but mostly not." I smiled at Dallas. "I have bits and pieces, but not much."

"God, that must have been hard," someone said.

I nodded and tried to lighten the mood. "I didn't even know where home was, but apparently I lived with this really good-looking guy who came to visit me at the hospital every day," I said, smiling at Dallas. "And there was a cat who was very happy to see me when I walked through the door."

They laughed, thankfully. And Jimmy raised his lemonade. "To the power of love. And to life. Thank you, Justin. And Dallas, for coming along today. It means a lot to me. I know we met in terrible circumstances, and I'm sorry for that. But you both showed me a great kindness in your forgiveness. Our door is always open to you, and you'll always have a seat at our table."

Oh wow. I wasn't expecting that, and I wasn't expecting to be so moved by his words. Dallas' hand squeezed mine just as another couple walked in through the side gate. The guy, about forty years old, was carrying an Esky and a camping chair, and as they said hello to everyone and a few jokes were made at their lateness, it was a welcome relief to have the attention off me.

Kathy gave me a sad smile. "Dad didn't mean to upset you. He's just a big ol' softy. He says mushy stuff all the time."

"No, it's okay. I just . . . I don't really have . . ." I cleared my throat. I couldn't finish that.

She seemed to understand because she nodded to the guy who had just arrived. "That's Steve. Dad found him at a truck stop when he was sixteen. Homeless, in trouble. Dad brought him home, sorted him out, and got him back into school," she said. "It's just what my parents do. They're good people."

I swallowed hard. "I can see that."

Just then, a line of younger kids came out of the house, each carrying a dish, plates, trays of meat, and different vegetable dishes, sauces, breads, and put them on the table. It was like a production line. "Lunch is served!" Nancy said, following the last kid out.

Everyone grabbed a plate and helped themselves. Dallas got mine for me, and before anyone began to eat, Jimmy stood with Nancy at the table. He put his arm around her, raised his lemonade, and said, "A full house is a full heart. And as always, compliments to the beautiful chef."

Everyone thanked Nancy and she waved her hand like it was nonsense, but it was pretty obvious she was proud to feed people. We all ate—the food was amazing—and talked quietly and laughed. The winter gods had blessed us with sun and warmth, and it was just a really lovely day.

Some of the guys asked us about the shop and Dallas was in his element talking about bikes and mechanical things, and yes, the caramel tart was amazing. But as much as I wanted to stay longer, my eyelids were beginning to betray me.

"I better get you home," Dallas said gently.

I nodded. "Yeah."

"Want me to get your scooter for you?"

"Nah. I'll be okay."

We said our goodbyes, and everyone said they'd see us 'next time' and it was funny because I was one hundred per cent sure there would be a next time. I really liked these people. Dallas helped me to my feet and held me while my head caught up. My leg didn't like the grass too much—it was too spongey—so Dallas took my arm and helped me walk to the concrete path.

"I'll walk you out," Jimmy said.

I thanked Nancy again for the food and Dallas helped me up the small step and inside. Jimmy held the door for me as we made it out the front of the house, and he walked at my pace to the ute. "Thanks again for coming," he said.

"Thanks for inviting us," Dallas replied. "It's been lovely."

"Sorry we can't stay," I said, knowing my words were slow. I hated that my brain did this when I was tired. "It's nap time for me."

Jimmy nodded and put his hand to my arm. "You need to look after yourself, son."

"Can I ask you something?" I asked.

"Sure."

"My compensation claim from the accident," I began. "Does that hurt you?"

"Hurt me?"

"Yeah. The money. I don't want you to lose money. Or your home. I don't want that."

"Ah," he said, finally clueing into what I meant. "No, it's all insurance. Don't you worry about that, Justin. My insurance company is dealing with all that, not me. I pay my insurance premiums and it was all deemed an accident so it was all covered."

I sighed. "Good. I was worried."

Dallas rubbed my back. "You don't need to worry about that, baby."

"Yes, I do."

Jimmy's smile faded. "Did you get your insurance sorted?"

"Yeah," Dallas said. "We just heard this week. The van's covered, and all medical bills."

Jimmy put his hand to his forehead. "Oh, thank heavens. You had me worried there for a second."

I smiled at him. The truth was, I still wasn't much good at thinking about money. I knew I should be, but it was all a bit too much. Another reason to be thankful for Dallas. He took care of me. He took care of everything. But my brain was starting to get fuzzy and my eyelids wouldn't stay open. "I'm tired."

Jimmy opened the ute door and Dallas helped me into my seat. "You don't be a stranger now," Jimmy said.

As we drove away, I sighed contentedly. I held my hand out for Dallas to hold, which he did. "I like them," I mumbled. "Good people."

"They are."

I closed my eyes, and the next thing I knew, we were home.

Dallas helped me up the stairs and he put me on the couch and took my boots off and I fell straight back to sleep. When I woke up, he was sitting with my feet in his lap flicking through rolled-up catalogues.

"Hey, handsome," I mumbled.

"Hey," he replied, smiling. "How you feeling?"

I thought about that for a second, took stock of my leg, my arm, my head. "I feel good." I held out my hand. "Help me sit up." He pulled me up to sitting, and I shook off any lingering remnants of sleep. "I need to pee."

He laughed and helped me to my feet, and when I came out of the bathroom, he was looking through the fridge. "Did you want something to drink?" he asked, collecting two bottled waters.

I leaned against the kitchen bench. "I just want to cuddle, if that's okay."

He grinned and stepped in front of me. "Always."

I opened my arms and he stepped into them. "How are you feeling today?" I asked.

He smiled against my neck. "I feel great today. Thank you for asking."

I chuckled but tightened my hold on him. "I love you, Dallas. You take care of me, and I dunno where I'd be if I didn't have you. I don't think I say thank you enough."

He gave me a squeeze and rubbed my back. "You don't have to thank me."

I pulled back so I could see his handsome face and those grey eyes that owned me. "Yes I do. I should thank you every day."

He kissed me sweetly. "You're welcome, baby."

"Today was a good day. Yesterday wasn't great, but today was. I really enjoyed us having lunch with Jimmy and his family. It felt good to be included in that."

Dallas smiled warmly. "It did. I wasn't sure what to expect, but they're very sweet."

"I want to see them again. If they ask."

He chuckled. "Okay. But I'm pretty sure your invitation is ongoing."

I sighed contentedly. "I know I can only take it one day at a time, and it's baby steps, according to Doctor Chang. But today was a good day and we should talk about the good days too. From now on, we should talk about the good things."

"We should," Dallas murmured. He studied my eyes, fixed my hair, and smiled. "You sound like you're talking about the future. And that's a real good thing, Juss."

The future, yes. Something I hadn't thought about much at all. "I've spent all this time trying to put my mind back together. Maybe I need to stop concentrating on the pieces that are missing," I admitted. "And start focusing on the pieces that I have."

Dallas' smile was breathtaking. "You talk about putting

the pieces of you back together, but Juss, you're also putting the pieces of me back together as well."

"The pieces of you?"

He nodded. "My heart broke into a million pieces the day of the accident. I thought I'd lost you. Then you woke up and didn't know who I was, and it broke all over again. But then you remembered my tattoos. You remembered me, and it meant so much. And every day since, you're getting better and stronger, and you look at me now like you used to look at me, and piece by piece, you're putting me back together."

I put my hands to his face. "All the pieces of you are perfect, Dallas."

He smiled and kissed my lips, my cheek, my eyebrow but he didn't speak.

"You said it sounded like I was starting to think of the future," I whispered. "And I guess I am. I didn't for a long time, but now . . . Now I can think of it. And I want a future with you. I can't think of my future without you in it."

Dallas pulled me against him, holding me tight, our bodies fitting together perfectly. I was safe in his arms, as he was in mine. "And just like that, Juss, you put another piece of me back together."

ABOUT THE AUTHOR

N.R. Walker is an Australian author, who loves her genre of gay romance. She loves writing and spends far too much time doing it, but wouldn't have it any other way.

She is many things: a mother, a wife, a sister, a writer. She has pretty, pretty boys who live in her head, who don't let her sleep at night unless she gives them life with words.

She likes it when they do dirty, dirty things... but likes it even more when they fall in love.

She used to think having people in her head talking to her was weird, until one day she happened across other writers who told her it was normal.

She's been writing ever since...

ALSO BY N.R. WALKER

Blind Faith

Through These Eyes (Blind Faith #2)

Blindside: Mark's Story (Blind Faith #3)

Ten in the Bin

Gay Sex Club Stories 1

Gay Sex Club Stories 2

Point of No Return – Turning Point #1

Breaking Point – Turning Point #2

Starting Point – Turning Point #3

Element of Retrofit – Thomas Elkin Series #1

Clarity of Lines – Thomas Elkin Series #2

Sense of Place – Thomas Elkin Series #3

Taxes and TARDIS

Three's Company

Red Dirt Heart

Red Dirt Heart 2

Red Dirt Heart 3

Red Dirt Heart 4

Red Dirt Christmas

Cronin's Key

Cronin's Key II

Cronin's Key III

Cronin's Key IV - Kennard's Story

Exchange of Hearts

The Spencer Cohen Series, Book One

The Spencer Cohen Series, Book Two

The Spencer Cohen Series, Book Three

The Spencer Cohen Series, Yanni's Story

Blood & Milk

The Weight Of It All

A Very Henry Christmas (The Weight of It All 1.5)

Perfect Catch

Switched

Imago

Imagines

Red Dirt Heart Imago

On Davis Row

Finders Keepers

Evolved

Galaxies and Oceans

Private Charter

Nova Praetorian

A Soldier's Wish

Upside Down

The Hate You Drink

Sir

Tallowwood

Reindeer Games

The Dichotomy of Angels

Throwing Hearts

Pieces of You - Missing Pieces #1

Titles in Audio:

Cronin's Key

Cronin's Key II

Cronin's Key III

Red Dirt Heart

Red Dirt Heart 2

Red Dirt Heart 3

Red Dirt Heart 4

The Weight Of It All

Switched

Point of No Return

Breaking Point

Starting Point

Spencer Cohen Book One

Spencer Cohen Book Two

Spencer Cohen Book Three

Yanni's Story

On Davis Row

Evolved

Elements of Retrofit

Clarity of Lines

Sense of Place

Blind Faith

Through These Eyes

Blindside

Finders Keepers

Galaxies and Oceans

Nova Praetorian

Upside Down

Sir

Tallowwood

Imago

Free Reads:

Sixty Five Hours

Learning to Feel

His Grandfather's Watch (And The Story of Billy and Hale)

The Twelfth of Never (Blind Faith 3.5)

Twelve Days of Christmas (Sixty Five Hours Christmas)

Best of Both Worlds

Translated Titles:

Fiducia Cieca (Italian translation of Blind Faith)

Attraverso Questi Occhi (Italian translation of Through These Eyes)

Preso alla Sprovvista (Italian translation of Blindside)

Il giorno del Mai (Italian translation of Blind Faith 3.5)

Cuore di Terra Rossa (Italian translation of Red Dirt Heart)

Cuore di Terra Rossa 2 (Italian translation of Red Dirt Heart 2)

Cuore di Terra Rossa 3 (Italian translation of Red Dirt Heart 3)

Cuore di Terra Rossa 4 (Italian translation of Red Dirt Heart 4)

Natale di terra rossa (Red dirt Christmas)

Intervento di Retrofit (Italian translation of Elements of Retrofit)

A Chiare Linee (Italian translation of Clarity of Lines)

Senso D'appartenenza (Italian translation of Sense of Place)

Spencer Cohen 1 Serie: Spencer Cohen

Spencer Cohen 2 Serie: Spencer Cohen

Spencer Cohen 3 Serie: Spencer Cohen

Spencer Cohen 4 Serie: Yanni's Story

Punto di non Ritorno (Italian translation of Point of No Return)

Punto di Rottura (Italian translation of Breaking Point)

Punto di Partenza (Italian translation of Starting Point)

Imago (Italian translation of Imago)

Il desiderio di un soldato (Italian translation of A Soldier's Wish)

Confiance Aveugle (French translation of Blind Faith)

A travers ces yeux: Confiance Aveugle 2 (French translation of Through These Eyes)

Aveugle: Confiance Aveugle 3 (French translation of Blindside)

À Jamais (French translation of Blind Faith 3.5)

Cronin's Key (French translation)

Cronin's Key II (French translation)

Au Coeur de Sutton Station (French translation of Red Dirt Heart)

Partir ou rester (French translation of Red Dirt Heart 2)

Faire Face (French translation of Red Dirt Heart 3)

Trouver sa Place (French translation of Red Dirt Heart 4)

Le Poids de Sentiments (French translation of The Weight of It All)

Lodernde Erde (German translation of Red Dirt Heart)

Flammende Erde 2 (German translation of Red Dirt Heart 2)

Vier Pfoten und ein bisschen Zufall (German translation of Finders Keepers)

Ein Kleines bisschen Versuchung (German translation of The Weight of It All)

Ein Kleines Bisschen Fur Immer (German translation of A Very Henry Christmas)

Weil Leibe uns immer Bliebt (German translation of Switched)

Drei Herzen eine Leibe (German translation of Three's Company)

Sixty Five Hours (Thai translation)

Finders Keepers (Thai translation)